In The Lamplight
She Lay There For A Few Seconds,
As If She'd Been Mummified,
Then Gave A Nervous Laugh.
Make That *Petrified.*

Of Nick?

No, she was being absurd. Nick would never physically hurt her. Realizing she was letting her nerves get the better of her, she sat up against the pillows, only just managing to cover herself with the sheet a moment before Nick opened the door.

His gaze flashed over her. "I see you're already in bed."

She blinked, suddenly confused. Should she have sat on the brocade chair instead? Or stood by the window? What was the protocol on the wedding night of a marriage of convenience?

"I thought this was where you'd want me."

"Oh, it is." An intense look filled his eyes. "I'd want you anywhere, Sasha."

Dear Reader,

I imagine it would be difficult being the middle child in a family. On the one hand you may not be given the greatest responsibility like the oldest, but then you aren't given as much leeway as the youngest either. You have to find your own place in the world.

And that's exactly what Nick Valente has done. Being the middle son in the dynamic Valente family has its own special challenges. As middle brother, Nick needed to find something for himself. He doesn't realize it at first, but his father's ultimatum to marry or lose the beloved family estate ends up being the best thing for Nick. It leads this middle son to finding true love with the one woman he can't forget—Sasha Blake.

I hope you enjoy this story, no matter your place in your own family.

Happy Reading!

Maxine

MAXINE SULLIVAN

THE C.O.O. MUST MARRY

Published by Silhouette Books
America's Publisher of Contemporary Romance

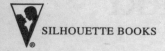

SILHOUETTE BOOKS

Recycling programs
for this product may
not exist in your area.

ISBN-13: 978-0-373-76926-1
ISBN-10: 0-373-76926-1

THE C.O.O. MUST MARRY

Copyright © 2009 by Maxine Sullivan

Visit Silhouette Books at www.eHarlequin.com

Printed in U.S.A.

Books by Maxine Sullivan

Silhouette Desire

The Millionaire's Seductive Revenge #1782
The Tycoon's Blackmailed Mistress #1800
The Executive's Vengeful Seduction #1818
Mistress & a Million Dollars #1855
The CEO Takes a Wife #1883
The C.O.O. Must Marry #1926

*Australian Millionaires

MAXINE SULLIVAN

credits her mother for her lifelong love of romance novels, so it was a natural extension for Maxine to want to write her own romances. She thinks there's nothing better than being a writer, and is thrilled to be one of the few Australians to write for the Silhouette Desire line.

Maxine lives in Melbourne, Australia, but over the years has traveled to New Zealand, the UK and the U.S.A. In her own backyard, her husband's job ensured they saw the diversity of the countryside, from the tropics to the outback, country towns to the cities. She is married to Geoff, who has proven his hero status many times over the years. They have two handsome sons and an assortment of much-loved, previously abandoned animals.

Maxine would love to hear from you and can be contacted through her Web site at www.maxinesullivan.com.

To Mum and Dad
"Love Forever"

One

"What are you saying, Dad?" Nick Valente asked his father, Cesare, as they sat on one of the terraced courtyards on the Valente estate.

"I'm saying I've been retired over six months now and while I've loved it here, this place is getting too big for us. Isabel and I have decided to move into an apartment in town."

The statement sucked the wind out of Nick. This place was *home*. He'd grown up on this estate in the Hawkesbury district of Sydney. His own mother had given birth to him here before taking off for greener pastures, leaving his father to meet Isabel six months later.

"The estate is yours," Cesare continued. "If you want it."

Something leaped inside him. Did his father even have to ask? Of course he wanted it. He wanted it so badly he had to turn his head away and look down over the cultivated lawns, lest his father see how *much* he wanted it.

And there was the crux of the matter.

He didn't trust his father.

Cesare was a crafty old devil who'd had a long reign as founder of The House of Valente, an Australian perfume dynasty now branching out in the rest of the world under the control of the eldest son, Alex, with their new perfume, "Valente's Woman." Cesare was used to getting his own way.

"And if I don't want it?" he said, playing it cool, just like he did every day in his job as Chief Operating Officer for the family business.

"Then I'll give it to Matt."

Damn.

He was close to Matt, but his younger brother liked living in the center of the city, and this place would end up neglected. Matt would die out here on the far outskirts of Sydney, no matter that he could commute.

He, on the other hand, would appreciate the break away from his city apartment and from the constant round of hard work and equally hard play.

He casually turned his head to look at his father. "Matt's never liked this place much," he pointed out coolly.

Cesare inclined his gray head. "I know that."

"So why give it to him?"

"I haven't…yet. It all depends on you."

His misgivings were increasing by the moment. "What's the catch, Dad?"

Cesare's lips twisted wryly. "You know me well." A calculating expression took over the older man's face. "You can have the estate on one condition. You have to get married."

Nick straightened in his chair. "What the hell!"

"This place needs a young family again."

"So I'm supposed to get married *and* have a family, too?" he said, sarcastically.

"That's usually the way it goes."

Nick shook his head. He had no plans to get married just yet. No woman was going to tie him down, and he'd be damned if he'd bring a child into the world whose parents didn't love each other.

"What about Alex and Olivia?" It was the most acceptable option to him. At least they would give this place the care it deserved.

"No, they have their own house now and wouldn't want to move. It would unsettle little Scott."

Yes, that was true. Alex and Olivia had adopted

eight-year-old Scott at Christmas. They wouldn't want to move again so soon, if at all.

Suddenly something clicked in Nick's brain as he looked at his father. "Tell me you didn't have anything to do with Alex marrying Olivia."

Cesare didn't even flinch. "I'd be lying if I said I hadn't."

Nick's mouth tightened. "Does Mum know what you've been up to?"

He'd always considered Isabel his mother. She was elegant, charming, loving, and quite formidable when riled. She'd been the only mother he'd known—until his real mother had started turning up during his childhood, causing havoc.

"Isabel and I have agreed to disagree. She knows my feelings on this, and I'm not about to change my mind. It's too important to me."

Nick swore. "Dammit, I'm not marrying some woman just to satisfy your perverted sense of power."

"Then Matt gets the estate."

His stomach tightened. "Matt won't want it once I tell him what game you're playing."

Cesare took a sip of his coffee before putting the cup down on the table. "Then I'll have to sell, won't I?"

Nick swallowed hard. His father thought he had it all figured out, did he?

"Just who the hell am I supposed to marry anyway? Should I just pick a woman from my Rolodex?"

"Sasha Blake."

Nick's brain stumbled. He hadn't thought about that name in years...hadn't thought about *her* in years...hadn't thought about that kiss.

Well, rarely.

"She isn't in my Rolodex," he snapped, not wanting to think about her at all. That kiss had been a minor lapse in judgment.

"She's perfect for you."

"I'm glad you think so."

Displeasure furrowed Cesare's brow, then cleared. "You'll see. Once you marry her you'll—"

"I'm *not* marrying her, Dad." If he was getting married—and he wasn't saying he would—*he'd* choose the woman. "Besides, isn't she in England?"

"No, she's back. She's an interior designer now, and I've asked her to redecorate this house."

The surprises just kept on coming, didn't they?

"This place is fine the way it is."

Cesare considered him. "You've always loved it here."

Nick shrugged. "It's home."

"And that's why I'm offering it to you."

"But only if I marry Sasha Blake, right?"

"It'll be good to join the two families. Porter and Sally Blake have been our friends for years."

"I've never trusted Porter." Sally was a nice enough woman, if a little too submissive.

"Forget Porter Blake. It's his daughter you're marrying."

"I'm not marrying anyone. Period."

There was a small pause. "Sasha will be here tomorrow morning checking things while we're in the city. It might be a good time to talk to her."

"No."

His father went very still. Then, "I think Matt will be more than happy to change the whole look of this place, don't you? And Sasha must have some innovative ideas she's picked up from living in London."

Nick swore. "Why are you doing this, Dad?"

Cesare looked at him, a hint of vulnerability in his eyes. "I've had one heart attack already. I want to see you married before I die."

"It was a mild heart attack," Nick rasped, remembering.

"And the next one may be fatal, *figlio mio*," *son of mine,* he said, lapsing into Italian.

Nick felt an inward shudder at the thought and knew his father had him right where he wanted him. He could fight Cesare on everything but this. That heart attack had really shaken up the whole family, and *he* wasn't about to be responsible for any further attacks.

Marrying to please his father may sound ridicu-

lous in this day and age, but he'd been raised with
strong family values. He'd do what was necessary.

But did it have to be Sasha Blake of all people he
had to marry?

A shapely female bottom and matching long legs
in white trousers greeted Nick when he opened the
front door to his parents' house the next morning.
They belonged to a gorgeous female figure standing
in strappy sandals on a chair near the staircase.

At least they were until the woman turned, saw
him and gave a squeal of fright, then started to topple
off. He raced forward and caught her as she fell back
into his arms.

For a moment she stared up at him. "Nick?" she
whispered, almost as if his name was a secret.

He looked down at the beautiful blonde and
wanted to lie and say no, he wasn't Nick. And he'd
never kissed her either. Nor did he want to again.

She was Trouble.

And he had to ask her to marry him.

"Hello, Sasha."

She continued to stare up at him with eyes good
at robbing a man of his thoughts. He'd forgotten the
impact of those long sweeping lashes featuring eyes
the color of green satin. Even when she was growing
up there was something about them that tried to

pierce his defenses. It had taken a constant and concentrated effort not to let her succeed.

Their kiss had come close.

"What on earth were you doing up there?" he growled, setting her on her feet, fascinated despite himself at the visible pulse beating at her throat and a faint blush dusting her cheeks. She'd been a pretty teenager before, but now she'd grown into a very beautiful woman.

She pushed against him and stepped back. "I thought I saw a crack in the wall, so I was checking it out."

The impact of her touch lingered. And so did the scent of her perfume—Valente's Woman. Somehow he was glad she wore his family's perfume.

"I hear you're an interior designer now," he said for something to say.

"Yes, I am." She seemed to pull herself together, and an excited light entered her eyes. "And I'm so happy your father chose me to redecorate this place."

Remembering, he shot her a dark look. "I don't want this house redecorated. It's fine how it is."

Disappointment crossed her face before she gave a tiny smile that held a touch of defiance. "Then it's as well this isn't your house, or I wouldn't have a job."

Tension rocked his stomach. "Look, let's go into the salon. I'll get Iris to make us some coffee."

Her expression grew wary. "I'm supposed to be working."

"Then add an extra hour's wages to the bill. My father can afford it."

She tipped her head to one side, her straight blond hair swaying like a sheen of silk over her shoulders. "You're very generous with your father's money."

"He wants me to talk to you."

She tensed. "Oh. I see. He's firing me, is he?"

"No, it's not that at all." But she was going to wish it was.

Relief fluttered across her face. "Then what can you possibly say to me that he can't himself?"

Marry me.

He opened his mouth to say it but realized it would be a bit too much all in the space of a minute. No need to break a record with this.

He gestured toward the salon. "The coffee first." He waited for her to precede him, then used the intercom to ask Iris to bring in some coffee.

When he turned to look at Sasha she was standing by the fireplace. Suddenly he couldn't take his eyes off her. It was crazy but she looked so right standing there in tailored white pants and a soft-knit green top, slim and refined and such a contrast amongst all this heavy, ornate furniture.

"It's not polite to stare."

Her words broke through his thoughts. "You're

different from what I remember." It was more than a physical difference, but he wasn't sure what it was yet.

Her eyelids flickered. "What do you remember, Nick?"

"Our kiss."

She gave a soft gasp. "It's not gentlemanly of you to bring that up."

"I was only being honest."

"Ever heard of being too honest?"

"I don't work like that."

"True. You were nothing less than honest after that kiss, weren't you?" she said, a wry twist coating her lips.

"If you mean that I didn't profess everlasting love, then you're right. I'd prefer not to sugarcoat things." It had been a kiss—a stunner of a kiss—but that's all it was. "Why, did I hurt your ego?"

"What? No way," she said quickly, perhaps too quickly. "It was my first kiss by a man, that's all. Up until then they'd all been boys."

"No doubt you've been plenty kissed since then."

"I'm not naive."

"Yes, I remember Randall. You had a fling with him, didn't you?"

Strangely, the thought of her with other men—with Randall Tremaine—had always unsettled him, but he forced himself to ignore it. She could kiss whomever she liked, make love to whomever she liked. And she had. It had nothing to do with him.

Until now.

She gave a shaky sigh. "I can't believe the first thing we talk about after seven years is kissing."

"I can."

A blush rose up her cheeks but just then Iris appeared in the doorway with the tray of coffee, interrupting the moment. They exchanged a few pleasantries, then Iris put the tray down on the coffee table and left the room.

"Shall I pour?" Sasha said, taking a seat on the sofa.

"Thanks." He sat down opposite, watching as she poured with an elegance that was innate. Once again he had the feeling she looked right in this setting. He grimaced to himself. Or perhaps it was just because his father had implanted the idea in him.

"So how long has it been since you left for London?" he asked as she passed him the cup and saucer.

"Five years."

"You were twenty when you left. That's young to be in a big city by yourself."

"I wasn't by myself," she said, and just for a moment his breath stopped at the thought of her living with another man. "I have an aunt who lives there, so I stayed with her for a few years. Then I got my own place." She picked up her own cup and saucer but didn't drink from it. "Our fathers are friends. I'm sure your father would have told you all this."

"He probably did," he said without thinking, angry at himself for caring even for a moment that she may have lived with some guy.

"But you didn't bother to listen, right?"

He didn't like being put on the spot like that. *He* was usually the one putting people on the spot. "It's been five years. I'd probably forgotten it long ago."

She held his gaze for a moment. "I'm sure." Her tone made him stiffen but before he could analyze her response, she put her coffee cup down on the table. "Now. Please give me the message from your father. I need to get back to work."

Fine. So did he.

He placed his own cup on the table, then leaned back on the sofa, giving himself a full view of her face. He needed to see her reaction. "It's not a message exactly. It's more a request."

Her smooth brow crinkled in a frown. "He wants me to do something?"

"Yes." He paused, trying to find the words that had been going over and over in his head all night. "Did he tell you he and my mother are moving into a smaller place in the city?"

She blinked in surprise. "No, he didn't." Her forehead cleared. "So *that's* why he wants me to re-decorate. He's planning on selling."

"No, he's not selling. He wants to keep it in the family. He wants *me* to have it."

Her eyes lit up, making her look even more beautiful. "Oh, that's wonderful, Nick. This place is gorgeous. I've always loved coming here."

Something wavered inside him. "Then perhaps you'd like to stay."

Her enthusiasm paused. "What do you mean? Rent it from you or something?"

"I mean share it with me."

"Sh…share it with you?" she all but squeaked.

"He wants me to marry you, Sasha."

She sucked in a sharp breath, then slowly let it out. "Good Lord."

His sentiments exactly. His father's ultimatum had been one of the few times in his life he'd had the rug pulled out from under him. He didn't like the feeling. Not one bit.

"Why?" she said in amazement after a moment or two.

"He wants to give me this house to carry on the Valente name but he knows I don't want to settle down so he's blackmailing me. If I don't marry you he'll give the house to Matt."

She shook her head. "No, this place doesn't suit Matt. It suits *you*."

He warmed to her.

"But Nick, I don't understand why he's chosen me for your wife."

He shrugged. "For some reason he thinks you're perfect for me."

Her eyes softened. "He does?" Then she stiffened and began to shift uneasily. "That's sweet of him, but we both know that's ridiculous. I've just come along at the right time, that's all."

"It seems that way," he agreed, happy to see she had a clear head on her shoulders. This was going to be easier than he'd expected. They wouldn't have to get mixed up with all the emotional trappings other married couples had to worry about.

"So what are you going to do, Nick?"

"Marry you."

The blood drained from her face but she soon gathered herself together. "Oh, really?"

He'd made up his mind to do this, and he didn't expect any resistance to the idea. "He's dead serious, Sasha. He wants a Valente to live in this house, and he wants our families to be joined."

She shook her head. "No, Nick."

"I don't like it any more than you do. Frankly, marriage was never in my cards. I like being single."

"So do I."

That surprised him. Career women or not, most of his lady friends had wanted more than a sexual relationship. Most had wanted marriage, despite their declarations that they didn't.

"You may not know this, but my father had a heart attack six months ago. It was only a mild one," he assured her, seeing her slight alarm, "but he's worried he'll have a major one and won't see me married before then. That's why he's come up with this plan."

"Nick, I'm sorry about his heart attack, but I can't do this."

His mouth tightened. "Then this place will go to Matt. I suggest you get ready for some heavy modernization when you redecorate."

She winced. "Talk to your father, Nick. He may let you marry someone else."

All at once he didn't want any other woman. "I know my father. He won't want anyone but you. He can be stubborn."

"So can I."

"Sasha, look—"

She sprang to her feet. "Nick, stop it." Then she straightened her shoulders, her eyes showing a spirit only hinted at while growing up. "Now, if you don't mind, I need to get on with the job, no matter whom the redecoration is for."

She hurried out the door, her high heels clicking on the timber floor as she headed down the hallway toward the kitchen.

Nick sat back on the sofa and contemplated what had just happened. There weren't many women who would actually refuse to marry him. Hell, he didn't think there were any.

But if he was getting married then so was Sasha Blake.

To him.

He just had to find a way to make it happen.

He smiled grimly. Making things happen was one thing a Valente did extremely well.

Two

Sasha finished taking measurements at the Valente mansion, then left as soon as she could. She kept expecting to turn around and find Nick there, ready to pressure her into marriage.

A marriage he didn't want.

And neither did she.

So why was she worried? With his father giving his stamp of approval she was just a convenience, that's all. Nick would go find someone else to marry, and Cesare wouldn't really care as long as it was someone suitable.

Of course if Nick *did* marry then she'd have to

work with Nick and his new wife to redecorate the house. Could she do it, knowing how much she'd been in love with him all those years ago?

Not that she was in any danger of loving him now.

No, it would be a matter of pride.

Unable to concentrate on any real plans for the redecorating until she knew what would happen to the estate, she spent the rest of the afternoon helping her mother around the house. She was preparing dinner around seven when her father walked into the kitchen earlier than usual.

In all the years she'd lived here previously, her father rarely got home before eight. Sasha suspected back then he hadn't always been working late, and that feeling hadn't abated since her return from London. She didn't know how her mother coped with it all.

"I never thought a daughter of mine would be so selfish," Porter Blake snapped with an accusing glare at her.

Sasha's forehead creased as she glanced across at her mother, then back to her father. "What do you mean, Dad?"

"Nick Valente. He asked you to marry him, didn't he?"

Her heart sank. Had Nick gone running to her father? "How did you know that?"

"Cesare told me. And you said *no*. For the love of God, why?"

She tried not to let him make her feel guilty. "I have that right."

"No, you don't. Your mother and I have given you everything, and you can't even do this one thing for us."

Sally Blake started toward him. "Porter, what are—"

"Be quiet, Sally," he all but growled.

Sasha hated the way he talked to her mother in private. In company, butter wouldn't melt in his mouth.

"Dad, don't speak to Mum that way."

Porter made a dismissive gesture. "This isn't about your mother and me. This is about you and Nick. Dammit, girl. It's not like Nick isn't a good-looking young man."

Sasha could only stare at him in dismay. "I don't understand why you want me to marry at all."

Her father's eyes darted away, then back again. "The Valentes are our closest friends. It would be nice to join the two families."

That was a crazy reason to get married. Nobody did that sort of thing anymore, or if they did *she* wasn't about to do it.

"Dad, I'm not going to marry a man I don't love just to bring two families together."

The wind seemed to leave Porter and he sat down

heavily on a chair, looking defeated. "If you don't, then say goodbye to this house and everything we have."

"What are you talking about?"

"If I don't close a deal with the Valentes soon, I'll lose my shipping business. If that happens we lose everything."

Sasha ignored her mother's gasp. "But Cesare's your friend. He'll give you the deal."

"He's a businessman first. If anyone undercuts my offer he'll go with them." He paused. "Unless you're his daughter-in-law and then he'll want to keep it in the family."

"You don't know what you're asking," she whispered.

Her father sighed heavily. "You're right, but it's the only chance we've got."

Sasha shook her head. No, she couldn't do it. It was too much to ask of her.

Then she caught her mother's pleading eyes. "Sasha, darling," Sally began. "Do you think it would be so terrible to marry Nick?"

She drew a painful breath. "Oh, Mum, no. Don't ask this of me."

"Darling, I have to. If not for your father's sake, then mine."

Sasha hated seeing how her mother always put her husband first, and no amount of talking on her part could change her mind. It was part of the reason she'd gone to London. She'd had to get away from her parents.

And from the memory of Nick Valente.

She sighed with defeat. "Do you have Nick's address?"

Her father's face lit up and so did her mother's. "No, but I can get it right now." He jumped to his feet, then hesitated. "Thank you, Sasha," he muttered, then strode out of the kitchen.

Sasha looked at her mother, who was blinking back tears of happiness. "Darling, I'm sorry. I know—"

"Mum, please don't say anything right now."

Her mother flushed. "Okay. If that's what you want."

"It is."

Sasha went to get her purse when her father came back with Nick's address. It was small comfort to know she could help her parents.

At what cost to herself she wasn't sure.

An hour later she stood in front of Nick's apartment and rang the doorbell. Right now the cost seemed much too high a price to pay.

Oh God, if only this had been seven years ago. She'd have given anything for him to ask her to marry him back then.

She remembered that kiss in the gazebo in the summer rain. It had just happened and she'd almost melted in a puddle at his feet. He'd surely felt everything she'd felt, she'd told herself as it ended and she'd moved in closer for another one. He'd realize he loved her and couldn't live without her and any moment he'd tell her so.

Instead he'd held her back from him, obviously appalled he'd kissed her. She'd seen it in his blue eyes that had turned from light blue to dark in a matter of seconds.

And then he'd left her there, gone back up to the main house to the party and casually taken another woman home, just like he'd been exchanging his Ferrari for another model. It had devastated her, but she'd never let him know it.

Right at that moment the door opened and Nick stood there, devastatingly handsome and undeniably male, and nothing on his handsome face giving away any of his thoughts.

He moved back to let her enter the apartment. "My father said you'd be stopping by."

"Word gets around fast."

She stepped through the doorway, trying to shake her feelings of the past. It was the present…now… that should concern her.

He gestured to the leather couch. "Make yourself comfortable. Would you like a drink?"

"No, I'm fine." She couldn't sit, and if she tried to drink anything she'd probably choke. Her throat ached with pure defeat.

His blue eyes rested on her. "So what made you change your mind?"

"My parents." She didn't want him to think it had been for any other reason. "I'm their only child and they really want our families to be joined." She swallowed hard. "I can't deny them that."

Cynicism twisted the corners of his mouth. "I'm sure your father's delighted."

Her heart thudded inside her chest. Could Nick know that her father's shipping business needed this deal?

Then she realized he didn't know. If he did, he'd have certainly blackmailed her into marriage. Nick wouldn't hesitate to use any leverage he could to get her to do what he wanted.

Still, she felt the need to defend her father.

She angled her chin. "Why do you say it like that?"

"Your mother's a nice woman. I'm sure she wouldn't pressure you into a marriage you don't want."

She realized he didn't know her mother that well. If her father wanted something, then her mother was usually the go-between.

He held her gaze. "I don't think I can say the same for your father."

"And that's so different from *your* father?"

Surprise flickered in his eyes. "True."

She briefly appreciated her feeling of triumph. "*Both* my parents are happy about this marriage, Nick."

He scrutinized her. "Why do I believe you?"

"Because it's the truth." She couldn't confess her mother was happy for Porter's sake, or Nick might get suspicious.

"Okay, let's get down to business. First, I want to assure you that if things don't work out we can always get a divorce later on."

She winced inwardly at his insensitivity, or his honesty, as he liked to call it. It was the same this morning when he'd asked if his rejection had hurt her ego in the gazebo that night.

Could a man be so hard-hearted to a young woman in love with him?

Hadn't he been able to tell she'd put her heart and soul into that kiss?

Of course he hadn't.

"Are you reassuring me or yourself?" she asked cynically.

He scowled. "I just don't want either of us to feel totally trapped."

"How nice."

He shot her a hard look, then, "Do you want children?"

Her heart skipped a beat and all her cynicism disappeared. "Do you?"

"One day. Not yet."

"Me, too." She hadn't thought about children. They were a lifetime commitment, and one that connected her to Nick for the rest of her life.

She wasn't sure she could do that.

Wasn't sure she *wanted* that.

He started toward a small table where there were a bunch of papers. "Right. Looks like we have a wedding to plan."

She took a quick breath. "Hold on. I have one condition of my own before we settle this."

He stopped to look at her, his eyebrow winging upward. "And that is?"

"You remain faithful to me," she said without hesitation. "I won't accept the humiliation of you having affairs. If you can't do it, tell me now."

Something shifted in his expression. "It's not that I can't do it. The question is whether I *want* to remain faithful."

She tensed. "I'd suggest you've probably had enough affairs to last a lifetime anyway."

"You know me so well," he drawled.

She raised her chin. "I'll accept nothing less, Nick."

There was a lengthy silence as their eyes held and locked. This was the one thing she wouldn't relent on, it was too important to her.

Then he expelled a breath. "You may be surprised

to know this but I do take marriage vows seriously, and mine especially. I can assure you I will remain faithful."

She let out a quiet sigh, but wasn't sure if it was relief or despair. Her only chance to refuse to marry him had just dissolved into thin air.

On the other hand, at least she could do this one thing for her mother. She had to keep remembering that.

"The wedding will be in three weeks."

She swallowed past her dry throat. "That soon?"

"The sooner we get this over and done with the better."

"Yes," she said, giving in to the inevitable.

She felt the same as Nick, but probably for different reasons. She suspected Cesare wouldn't let his sons sign the deal for her father until after their marriage vows had been taken. Cesare wasn't a fool.

If only he was.

Nick was pleased with himself after Sasha left his apartment. He'd known he wouldn't have to do a thing except tell his father she had refused his offer. Cesare had immediately got on the phone to Porter and offered regrets that they wouldn't be in-laws.

And that's all that was needed. Porter knew what side his bread was buttered, and the last thing he would want was to offend Cesare.

Nick gave a snort of derision. Porter Blake was a

wimp. If the Valente family didn't have money, the other man wouldn't be hanging around being Cesare's friend. No, Porter would be out with his latest lady friend. The man was a rake of the worst kind, his affairs the worst-kept secret.

No wonder Sasha was insisting on fidelity in their marriage. She had to know about her father's numerous affairs.

Or did she?

He hadn't asked her straight out in case she didn't know. Not that he was protecting Porter. It was merely that if Sasha didn't know, then he wasn't about to tell her.

He only hoped he didn't live to regret giving his word. Women were notorious for having an angle for everything, and he suspected Sasha did, too.

Was she marrying him for reasons other than her family?

More prestige?

More money?

Better contacts for her work?

Time would tell, but he'd be ready for her if that happened. No one pulled the wool over his eyes. If they did, it didn't happen a second time.

Three

At eighteen Sasha had dreamed about a white wedding to Nick in a beautiful church in Sydney— the perfect setting for their perfect love for each other.

Now at twenty-five, a stylish ceremony on the sun-drenched lawn of the massive Valente estate was more than lovely, but a marriage of convenience to a man who'd never given her a moment's thought wasn't quite the same.

And that was never more prominent than on her wedding day. She'd been nervous in her responses throughout the ceremony but Nick hadn't missed a beat. Obviously she still didn't affect him in the slightest, least of all by marrying him.

"I now pronounce you man and wife."

Oh God. Sasha's knees threatened to wobble, making her grateful for her white wedding gown hiding them from view.

"You may now kiss the bride."

She swallowed hard as she turned to fully face Nick, looking so handsome in his black tuxedo. She'd melted the last time he'd kissed her all those years ago but until his lips were on hers again she wouldn't know for sure how she'd react.

His blue eyes gave nothing away as he lowered his head. Their lips touched and Sasha nervously held her breath, waiting for something…anything… to kick in. It was pleasant, but she didn't melt.

Thank God!

He broke off the kiss and they stared at each other. She was so relieved that she broke into a small smile. His eyes narrowed, making her wonder what he was thinking.

Everyone started to clap, bringing the world back into focus. She turned toward their beaming guests seated on the largest of the private courtyards surrounding the main house. Everyone loved a wedding, it seemed.

Everyone but the bride and groom.

People surrounded them with congratulations

and before too long a string quartet began playing music and waiters started circulating with glasses of champagne.

"You've made your mother and me very happy, Sasha," her father said, kissing her cheek, pride shining from his eyes. It was silly but despite everything, Sasha felt teary that she'd done something to make her father proud of her.

"We're so glad," Nick responded, his voice holding a touch of sarcasm.

His words spoiled the moment for Sasha and she blinked the moisture out of her eyes in time to see Cesare send Nick a warning glance. She wondered again why Nick didn't like her father.

Cesare leaned forward and kissed her on the cheek. "Isabel and I are very happy, too," he said, speaking for his wife, who was seeing to their guests. Then he slapped Porter on the back. "We're all one big happy family now, *amico mio*."

And Porter beamed. "Yes, our two families have been joined together at last, my friend."

Sasha swallowed back a hysterical comment that perhaps her father should have married Nick, but then she saw her mother's happy face and forced herself to relax.

She had done this for her mother.

After that the late afternoon rolled into evening, drawing the hours closer to when she and Nick would be alone. Thankfully their two hundred guests kept her occupied and stopped her thinking about it too much.

"Everything's gone very smoothly, don't you think?" Isabel asked, rescuing Sasha from an older relative and leading her over to the tables laden with wedding gifts beside the open French doors.

Sasha really liked her new mother-in-law. Isabel had always been one of her favorite people. "You've done wonders, Isabel. Thank you so much. I know it took a lot to get it all done in time, especially when you had to move into your new apartment, as well."

Isabel looked pleased. "Anything for you, Sasha. And Nick, of course." Then as quickly she frowned. "I still don't condone what Cesare has done, but after his heart attack I don't want to upset him too much. I've tried all I can, but he's a law unto himself."

Sasha had appreciated it when Isabel had taken her aside two weeks ago and asked her if she knew what she was doing. The other woman had known her husband was blackmailing Nick into marrying her and for a while she'd been very vocal about it.

Knowing she had to do this, Sasha had hurriedly assured her it was okay, and things had proceeded with alarming speed.

"Being a law unto themselves seems to be a trait of the Valente men," Sasha said.

"Yes. And Nick has assured me he knows what

he's doing." She squeezed Sasha's arm. "I'm so happy to have you in the family."

"Thank you," Sasha said huskily. It was lovely to be welcomed so warmly. If she and Nick were truly in love…

"And you know," Isabel's voice cut through Sasha's thoughts, "when I see how happy Alex and Olivia are now, it appears that Cesare knows what he's doing."

Sasha regarded Nick's older brother across the courtyard. Alex was here today with his wife and their adopted eight-year-old son, Scott. Olivia was the daughter of movie legend, Felicia Cannington, and was just as beautiful as her famous mother, and more than gracious. The love between Alex and Olivia made Sasha catch her breath.

Yet just because last year Cesare had black-mailed Alex into marrying Olivia and somehow the two had fallen in love didn't mean it would work for her and Nick.

It wouldn't.

For love to grow there had to be a basic need for love within that person. Nick had no need for love from any woman, and especially not *her*.

"They certainly look very happy," Sasha agreed, keeping quiet about her thoughts. Isabel loved Nick and only wanted the best for her second stepson she'd raised since he was a baby.

Isabel nodded. "You know, I don't think Nick got

any sympathy from Alex about it all." She gave a wry smile. "Especially when he's marrying *you*."

Sasha forced herself to smile back. She didn't think of herself as a beauty, but she knew her looks were probably the only thing she had going for her with Nick.

"Matt must be getting worried that he's next," Sasha said, trying to take the focus off herself.

A worried gleam entered Isabel's eyes. "He says he's not. He told his father he wouldn't be coerced into anything. Of course, when Cesare wants something..." she trailed off, just as Nick came strolling up to them.

"Somebody wants something, Mum?" Nick said, coming up next to them with a smile that must be more for Isabel, Sasha decided. If he ever smiled at her like that...

"Me. I need a drink," Isabel quipped, shooting her new daughter-in-law a look that said it was time to move on. Sasha wanted to beg her not to leave, but that would look foolish.

"I'll do that for you," Nick offered, about to turn away.

"No, honey, that's fine. I want to see your father anyway. I need to make sure he's taken his medication."

The line of Nick's mouth tightened at the mention

of his father. It was easy to see he hadn't forgiven Cesare for all this.

And rightly so. *Both* their fathers had a lot to answer for, Sasha knew. It was the one bond they had in common.

Nick turned the charm on for some of their guests who had come up to say they were leaving. A charm that wasn't false but neither was it for her benefit.

Still, she gratefully accepted the distraction to say goodbye, fielding more questions about not having a honeymoon. No one had dared ask about the haste of their marriage, but if they thought she was pregnant they'd soon find out she wasn't.

And if they wondered about the lack of affection between her and Nick? Maybe then they would guess the hasty marriage was for convenience. She didn't want anyone thinking it was for love.

Certainly not Nick.

Once all their guests had departed, Sasha left Nick talking to Matt beside his Aston Martin, but not before she saw the scowl on Nick's face and suspected he was probably warning his younger brother to watch out for their father. Though by the confident set of his head, Matt wasn't too concerned for his future.

She almost felt sorry for Matt. Just as no doubt Nick was feeling sorry for *himself* right now for having to marry *her*. She felt an instant's hurt but quickly dismissed it.

She had to keep busy.

Walking into one of the smaller dining rooms, she began tidying up, gathering the few remaining glasses and stacking them at one end of the table for the caterers to collect. It had been a good idea of Isabel's to use the room for some elderly relatives as a quiet place to get away from all the commotion and noise of the wedding.

And didn't she know exactly how they felt? If only she could have hidden in here permanently, away from Nick, away from the night ahead.

"Leave it."

Her head shot up to find Nick standing in the doorway. Panic stirred inside her chest. "But—"

"The catering crew will clean up."

"I know but—"

"You'll get that beautiful dress dirty," he pointed out, his enigmatic gaze pausing over her.

"Oh." She glanced down at the smooth white satin of her simply styled wedding dress. She'd been so anxious she'd totally forgotten she was wearing it. Any other bride would be horrified at the treatment.

Of course, who could call her a typical bride?

"Come on," he said brusquely, interrupting her thoughts. "Let's go upstairs. Iris will see everything is put right here."

Swallowing hard, she placed the glass down on

the table and started to walk toward him. "Has Matt gone?" she said for something to say.

His jaw clenched. "Yes."

Then he cupped her elbow and led her up the sweeping staircase, his touch sending a shiver through her that she tried to ignore. There would be more touching soon, more exploring, molding her softer curves to his hard body.

"Relax. You look like you're going to the guillotine."

"Maybe I've already lost my head," she quipped.

His eyes narrowed as he glanced sideways at her. "What does that mean?"

She blinked. Oh heavens. He surely didn't think she was talking about love?

"Nothing, except that I'd have to be crazy to marry you, that's all."

A moment crept by while they continued up the stairs and she held her breath but he said nothing further.

Soon they came to one of the large bedrooms they would use until she could renovate the master bedroom. The bed had already been turned back for them.

Suddenly she felt overwhelmed and she hung back in the doorway. Part of her wanted to know what making love with Nick would be like. Another part of her wanted to run for the hills.

Nick walked over to the large windows and stood looking out for a few seconds, his back to her. "Come here."

Her breath stopped. This was it.

Not wanting to appear childish or afraid, she started across the plush carpet but when she got close he didn't reach for her as expected.

He stood looking out over the estate's magnificent lawns and gardens deeply shadowed by the setting sun.

"Thank you for helping me keep all this," he murmured, the rough edge of emotion in his voice.

Oh.

Pleasure swept through her. "You belong here, Nick."

He turned and put his hand under her chin, lifting her face up to him. "That's the nicest thing anyone has ever said to me."

And then his lips descended.

She wasn't expecting it right then and she didn't have time to prepare. All at once he was there and the second his mouth touched hers she slid into his kiss. It was soft and slow and she melted for him like a frost in the morning sun.

Just as unexpectedly, he took the kiss deeper, pulling her with him into a world she'd dipped into only once before, many years ago. It was a world that tilted on its axis and began to spin out of control.

His tongue gave her strokes of pleasure, his hands sliding down to her hips and pulling her up against him, his body telling her he was a man who wanted, and that she was the woman to give.

And then he eased back.

And the world righted itself…slightly.

He lifted a strand of hair off her cheek. "Want to take a shower?" he asked huskily, his blue eyes holding a dark glitter.

"Er…together?"

He eased into a smile. "Is that an offer?"

She felt her cheeks wash with pink. "No."

He leaned back further, his eyes softening with understanding. "You're shy?"

She swallowed past her dry throat. "Only the first time," she whispered, hoping he'd take the hint so she wouldn't have to say it in words.

"And after that?" he teased.

"I don't—"

He chuckled and stepped back before she could finish. "Don't worry. I'll shower in my old room so that you can have some privacy." He strode away but stopped at the door and looked over his shoulder, his eyes no longer teasing. "This time."

Sasha stood there until she no longer heard his muffled footfall on the carpet along the landing.

She slowly exhaled. Oh God. How could she

know if she would be shy after she made love with him? She'd never made love with any man.

She was a virgin.

And a virgin who'd never felt anything for any man what she had felt for Nick all those years ago.

Nick whose kiss had blown her away just now. How could their wedding kiss earlier today have felt so different…so mild…yet this one be so mind-blowing?

This was like the kiss in the gazebo.

And unlike the episode after the gazebo, Nick wouldn't be going off with another woman. *She* would be the woman in his bed tonight. And all the nights ahead.

For now.

With a shaky hand she managed to unzip her dress and step out of it, carefully placing it over a chair. Then she headed for the shower, aware she was leaving behind more than her wedding dress. Tonight she was going to be a married woman in every sense of the word.

But would Nick even notice?

Or care?

Thankfully, when Sasha came out of the bathroom Nick was nowhere to be seen. Feeling awkward, she took off her silk robe and slipped beneath the covers in her nightgown, pulling the sheet up to her chin.

In the lamplight she lay there for a few seconds

looking like she'd been mummified, then gave a nervous laugh. Make that *petrified*.

Of Nick?

No, she was being absurd. Nick would never physically hurt her. Realizing she was letting her nerves get the better of her, she sat up against the pillows, only just managing to cover herself with the sheet a moment before Nick opened the door.

His gaze flashed over her. "I see you're already in bed."

She blinked, suddenly confused. Should she have sat on the brocade chair instead? Or stood by the window? What was the protocol on one's wedding night of a marriage of convenience?

"I thought this was where you'd want me."

"Oh, it is." An intense look filled his eyes. "I'd want you anywhere, Sasha."

"That wasn't what I meant."

"It's *exactly* what I meant."

"Nick—" She stopped speaking as he came toward her carrying a bottle of champagne and two glasses. He wore a navy bathrobe, his long legs bare and masculine. She could feel herself grow hot.

"I like the way you're looking at me," he said huskily.

Her gaze darted away, then back as she tried to get some sort of mental balance. "It feels strange being here like this with you," she said, her excuse lame but all she had.

"Why?"

She should tell him now.

She took a deep breath. "Perhaps because I—"

"Hell, you don't think of me like a brother, do you?"

His question took the wind from her sails. She blinked. "No." That was the last way she'd ever think of him. Hadn't those two mind-blowing kisses told him that, if seven years between?

"That's a relief." He was joking but she knew the question had been partly serious.

He held out a glass of champagne toward her. "Here, this should help you relax a little."

Grateful for something to do, she accepted it and took a sip, letting the bubbles slide down her dry throat. Perhaps drunk was the way to go, she mused, then dismissed the thought. If she were drunk she might say too much.

He sat down beside her on the bed, a sudden predatory gleam in his expression. "Why did you look shocked after I kissed you before?"

So he'd noticed she'd been taken aback by the power of that kiss.

"Um…at the wedding?" she said, deliberately misunderstanding him.

"No, not that placid little kiss I gave you at the

wedding ceremony. I mean the one just before by the window over there."

She cleared her throat, then decided on the truth. "I guess I didn't expect to…enjoy it so much."

"I did."

"Nick, I—"

"Have the most delectable looking mouth I've ever seen," he murmured, then put his glass down on the table beside the bed and did the same with hers. He leaned toward her. "I want to taste it again."

She moistened her lips, wanting to tell him about being a virgin but a mere second later his mouth settled on hers and she forgot everything but him. He nibbled on her lips until she sighed with delight, then took advantage by slipping his tongue inside.

In one swoop he was a part of her.

She shuddered. The kiss deepened and stole the breath from her lungs, sending excitement zinging to every pore in her body. She'd never known a kiss to be so all-inclusive.

And then he slowed the kiss and edged back a little to stare into her eyes, probing even. "There's something very unusual about you, Sasha."

She held her breath. Had he guessed?

"You haven't slept with many men, have you?"

"Um…no." She swallowed. "Does it make a difference?"

"Oh, yes," he rasped.

She couldn't read his expression and suddenly she was terrified he *wouldn't* make love to her if he knew she was a virgin. And that would be the biggest waste of her life. She was married to him, yes. And they would make love eventually, yes. But she'd missed out on her dream wedding. She didn't want to miss out on her honeymoon, too.

Not tonight.

"Kiss me, Nick."

A light flared in the back of his darkened eyes. Without hesitation, his mouth found hers again and he kissed her with a hunger that filled her with new awe. This kiss took her to places she'd never been before. She didn't want it to end.

She held her breath, her heart tilting with relief as he feathered kisses along her chin and down her throat. She couldn't bear him to leave her now.

He placed his lips at the center of her cleavage and murmured, "I've always thought your name suited you. Soft, sexy Sasha."

She shivered, never expecting this man would say something like that to her. It was the talk of a lover…a soon-to-be-lover.

He moved back and slid the thin strap of her nightgown off her shoulder, exposing one of her breasts to him. His hot gaze lingered on her for a long moment. She gasped when he began tracing her nipple with his fingertip, then held it between his fingers for his mouth to take over.

He suckled, and she almost came apart. She'd never realized her breasts were so sensitive to touch…to Nick. Oh God, this was *Nick* making love to her. *Nick* drawing on her nipple with his mouth. *Nick* who was sending such delicious sensations rippling through her. Everything he did, every move he made, was overshadowing everything else in the world.

The suckling continued, and she felt an odd sort of curl start at her toes and run its way upward. It tightened as it climbed higher through her thighs…higher and tighter still as it reached the core beneath her panties. She stiffened as something marvelous took hold and held her there, making her exhale in little gasps that seemed in rhythm with her body.

It was over almost before it began, the tightness diminishing, then disappearing as quickly.

Nick was looking at her curiously. "Did you just climax?"

"I…I think so. A little." She could feel herself blush. She wasn't sure. "Can we turn out the light, please? I'm embarrassed."

"No need to be embarrassed. Nothing should embarrass a man and a woman when they make love."

"The light, Nick. Please."

"No, I want to see you. I *need* to see you, sweetheart. All of you." And with that he took the hem of her nightgown and lifted it over her head.

Lamplight shone through the room, showing her naked body to him for the first time. "Beautiful," he murmured, reaching out and resting the palm of his hand on her stomach, leaving it there as if soaking up the touch of her skin. Her pulse shimmied through her veins, building anticipation. She wanted him to touch her more.

So much more.

Instead he leaned down and placed his lips against her *there* and just as she recovered from the shock of it, he gave a deep groan and pushed himself off the bed.

Her gasp was not because he'd left her, but because he was shrugging out of his bathrobe. In the blink of an eye her focus was on him, her sensibilities shocked at seeing a man in his full glory for the first time. Transfixed, she reached out to touch him. She could see her hand shaking but once she slid around him, he was her rock.

The air grew thick.

"Sasha," he said in a guttural voice.

She thrilled to the sound of him, to the sight of him, and now if she could just keep on…

"I need to touch you, Nick."

He made a low sound deep in his throat and that

was all the encouragement she needed. Tentatively she ran the tip of her finger over the head of his erection. She wanted to see what power she had over him.

He jerked. "No more," he growled and took her hand off him, twisting away to take a condom out of the bedside drawer and roll it on himself, entrancing her by his very masculine action. She'd read about all this in magazines, but the reality was overwhelmingly intimate.

"Slide over," he ordered, and he joined her on the bed, where he grasped her waist and rolled her on top of him.

She felt a rush of heat at the full length of his body against her own for the first time, and the feel of his hands cupping her bottom.

Their eyes met.

She wanted to look away but couldn't. Not when she could feel that curl starting in her toes again, making her want to tighten her legs and grind herself against him.

Suddenly he rolled her over and slid on top of her like he was meant to be there. And then he nudged her legs apart and pushed inside her a little.

She winced at the slight pain.

He stilled, his eyes widening in shock. "You're a *virgin?*"

She wanted to deny it. Wanted to say that she was

experienced so he would keep making her feel this way. Only she couldn't lie.

"Yes."

He swore but amazingly didn't pull out. He took a deep breath and then began to move slowly, his eyes never leaving her face. Carefully he filled her, and when he was fully inside her he stopped.

"Okay?" he asked hoarsely.

She nodded, too emotional to be able to speak. Nick had made her a woman.

His woman.

He began to move, and the world faded away. No one else existed, and nothing mattered. It was just the two of them, and when she climaxed Nick followed, and they came together in their own private world.

After Nick returned from the bathroom he sat on the bed and took her hands in his. "Why?"

Sasha swallowed. "Why didn't I tell you? You said it would make a difference and I…well…I wanted you to make love to me."

His mouth softened with tenderness. "You silly goose. The difference would have been in the way I made love to you, not in whether I made love to you at all."

"Oh."

"Your first time needs to be handled gently." A moment later he grimaced.

She saw the hint of regret in his eyes. "Nick, you were very gentle with me. Thank you."

He kissed her briefly. "Thank you for saying that." Then he leaned back with a penetrating look in his eyes that made her uneasy. "I seem to remember you telling me that you'd slept with Randall Tremaine."

She'd been prepared for this.

"Yes, I did say that. But I was eighteen, and I didn't want you thinking our kiss meant anything to me so…" she lifted one shoulder in a shrug, "I made it up."

"You were saving face?"

"Yes."

He considered her. "Why haven't you ever slept with anyone?"

"Perhaps I wanted to save myself for my husband."

A tic beat in his jaw. "And I've taken that away from you."

"No!" She swallowed, feeling bad for him. "Nick, look, we've both lost a lot of things from this marriage but we've gained some things, too. I'm glad you were my first, okay?"

His gaze took on a piercing look that held hers for long moments. Then just as quickly it changed to a sensual warmth that made her heartbeat stutter.

He got off the bed and scooped her from the sheets. "Nick! Where are you taking me?"

"To the shower."

She didn't ask why. It became obvious when he stood her in the cubicle and began to wash her with tenderness and care, and with a gentleness that almost brought tears to her eyes. This rich, arrogant playboy had a capacity for caring she hadn't really expected.

Then his hand and fingers replaced the soap, creating a lather that had nothing to do with bathing and everything to do with making love.

Four

For a moment Nick was confused when he woke up the next morning. He could hear car doors shutting and voices talking, and usually he didn't hear those sorts of noises from his tenth-floor apartment in the city.

Then he remembered.

He was married now. And this wasn't his apartment. He was at the Valente estate and the sounds he heard were the caterers clearing up the last of the wedding reception.

Sasha!

He lifted his head to find himself weighted to the bed by the naked female sleeping against his chest.

He looked down at the top of her blonde hair, and heat surged through his veins.

God, she'd been a virgin.

Amazingly there was something totally satisfying about knowing *he* was the only man to ever touch her like he had. Knowing he was the first man to be inside her like he'd been. He'd never thought he'd be the sort of guy who indulged in that sort of thing. He wasn't usually some sort of he-man who beat his chest in triumph.

Yet this time he wanted to do exactly that.

A virgin, for Pete's sake!

And of course that meant she'd lied to him all those years ago when she'd told him she'd gone out and slept with Randall Tremaine. It had been a few weeks after the gazebo incident and at the time he'd put it down to the fickle ways of a woman not knowing her own mind.

It hadn't stopped him wanting to knock the other man out when he'd seen them talking together briefly at a party. He remembered thinking Randall had been playing it so cool. No wonder. The poor guy had been an innocent pawn in it all.

Totally innocent.

Just like Sasha.

Hell, was he blind or what? Everything had pointed to her being a virgin, only he hadn't been looking. He'd just thought her a little inexperienced.

He could see it all now. The shyness in her, her first climax, wanting the light turned off.

The thought of being inside her again made him groan softly, and he knew he could wake her up and take her again. And it would be good for both of them.

Damn good.

But this wasn't a woman he could make love to, then kiss goodbye. This was his *wife*.

That thought had him easing out of bed and heading for the shower. He'd already given up his freedom for this marriage. He wasn't giving up his work, too.

But tonight…yes, tonight…he was going to enjoy teaching Sasha more about making love with a man.

Sasha opened her eyes to find the sun streaming in through the windows and an empty bed next to her.

She was a woman in every sense of the word now. And her heart was still intact.

She'd been terrified last night. Deep-down terrified that somehow Nick's lovemaking would open up the floodgates on the love she'd had for him years ago. It had been a very real fear.

But she'd had nothing to worry about, thank heavens. Nick's expertise in bed had made it so very special for her, and while lingering memories of her teenage love may have played a part in her enjoyment, pure physical attraction had saved the day.

It was such a relief!

Yes, she could cope with a physical relationship, she mused, throwing back the sheets and taking a couple of steps, then felt herself blush at how pleasurably sore her body was in all the places he'd touched.

And kissed.

Her hot shower should have soothed her but she kept remembering Nick carrying her in here last night. The thought of it brought a lump to her throat. How gentle he'd been.

And caring.

By the time she was dressed she was ready to face the day. The main thing was that she didn't love Nick nor had he guessed she'd been in love with him years ago.

And that was something to celebrate, she decided, as she went down the staircase to the kitchen. Today was business as usual for her husband, and it would be for her, too. She had her own work to do.

She had plans.

Lots of them.

Her fingers itched while she ate breakfast on the terrace, her mind racing with excitement, eager now to get back to the designs she'd started a few weeks ago.

The house was an interior designer's dream. It had a grand salon with picture windows and French doors looking out over spectacular gardens and courtyards. There was also a formal dining room and family living areas with five bedrooms and bathrooms, a study upstairs and one downstairs, and a kitchen with modern conveniences in an old-fashioned style.

Before too long she'd spread herself out in the downstairs study, her ideas and thoughts spilling onto the paper, her enthusiasm for the project continuing to bubble as she worked past lunch.

"Have you been here all day?" Nick said from the doorway.

Startled, she looked up and her heart skipped a beat at the sight of him. He was so handsome, and she'd been intimate with him last night. The thought made her feel warm all over.

She quickly dragged her gaze away to her watch. "Is it six o'clock already?"

He started to scowl as he stepped into the room and came toward her. "You're working on plans for the redecorating?" A muscle ticked in his cheek. "So you're still going ahead with it?" he asked, stopping in front of the desk.

That warm feeling disappeared at his tone. She

leveled him a look. They hadn't discussed it further, but she'd assumed he would still let her redecorate. "I guess that's up to you. You're the boss."

His eyes narrowed. "This is your home, too, now, you know."

"I guess it is."

Not for a moment did she think she owned this house. How could she? It was Nick's. It would always be Nick's even if she stayed married to him for fifty years.

Her breath stopped at the thought.

He leaned over the paperwork and looked at her plans for the main dining room. A minute later he grudgingly admitted, "They're good."

Despite herself, she felt a thrill at his praise.

She shrugged. "They're just ideas. There's still a lot to be done."

He studied her. "This means a lot to you, doesn't it?"

"Yes."

There was a tiny pause. "Fine. Then you have carte blanche to do what you like."

"Really?" Excitement rushed through her, but she quickly reined it in and said more primly, "Thank you."

"But my old bedroom stays as is."

"Oh?" She didn't say she'd planned to turn his room and the one next to it into a larger suite. "If that's what you want."

"It is."

"Okay." She'd allow him that. After all, she had the rest of the house.

"I'm going to shower and change before dinner," he said, a possessive gleam in his eyes sweeping over her, making her panic.

She swallowed. Was he asking her to join him?

"Um…I want to finish something here first. I'll freshen up in a minute."

A knowing look in his eyes, he turned toward the door. "Don't be too long."

"I won't."

They both knew she wasn't about to follow him upstairs. As much as she suspected being in his arms was addictive, she had to keep her distance or risk becoming his sex slave.

She smiled to herself. Would that be so bad?

Reality returned. Perhaps she ought to remind herself that she hadn't even warranted an "I'm home, honey" kiss. Whether he wanted her in his bed or not, it was clear he wasn't going to treat her like a real wife outside the bedroom. Not when they were alone anyway.

Shades of her parents' marriage?

No, she wouldn't think that.

The thought was too painful to contemplate. Sasha looked down at her designs and started working on them again. Work had always helped her concentrate on the moment, holding unhappy thoughts of the past or the possibility of a lonely future at bay. Work had been her salvation.

Now, if only she could get the color just right for…

"Dinner's almost ready," Nick said, startling her again.

She looked up and saw he'd showered and changed and she wrinkled her nose at herself. "I totally forgot the time again, didn't I?"

"Obviously you're not falling over yourself to be with me?" he drawled, not looking in the least put out about that.

No doubt he'd have plenty of women who *would* fall over themselves to be with him, she mused. Well, she wasn't one of his women.

She held her head high. "No, I'm not."

He considered her. "You're not like other women, are you?"

Was that a compliment? She wasn't sure.

"I guess not."

His face closed up. "You've got ten minutes," he said gruffly before striding away.

For a moment she just stood there. What was all that about? Her virginity? Was he feeling guilty about it? There was no need.

After that she hurried to shower and re-apply a light coating of make-up, leaving her straight blonde hair to fall loose past her shoulders. Taking her cue from Nick's dark trousers and polo shirt, she didn't dress up too much for dinner, instead slipping on a summery dress made from soft material that fell just above her knees.

Fifteen minutes later she joined him in the dining room. The hint of pleasure in his eyes made her heart race as she walked to where he held the chair out for her.

They sat down at the table. Iris served dinner before mentioning that Cesare had called to remind him about the English launch of "Valente's Woman." Then the older woman left them to eat.

Sasha was curious. "When is the U.K. launch?"

"In a couple of weeks."

"It'll do well over there."

He nodded. "It'll do well everywhere."

She had to smile at that.

"What are you smiling at?" he asked.

"Your arrogance."

His mouth quirked at the corners. "It's the Valente way."

"I know."

Some lazy moments passed while they ate in silence. Sasha was still amazed she was now actually married to Nick Valente. Who would have thought it?

Not her.

Aware she needed to move away from such

thoughts, she made herself reflect on how much effort went into launching a new perfume. "You should go with Alex. He may need you with him."

"Alex can handle it. He and Olivia will make sure it goes off with a bang."

All at once she didn't want him staying home for her sake. "Just because we're newly married doesn't mean you have to stay home with me."

His lips twisted. "Are you trying to get rid of me so soon?"

"Of course not. I'm just thinking you have other commitments and being married shouldn't change that."

He held her gaze for a moment, then, "If I thought Alex needed me, I'd go. But he doesn't and frankly, I'd prefer to stay home."

She noted he didn't say "stay with *her*."

Strangely she was rather glad he wasn't going away and leaving her alone. She seemed to have had too much aloneness these past few years.

Had he?

She didn't think so.

They began to talk about the wedding—was it only yesterday?—and before too long Iris was serving dessert, and then not long after, they finished their dinner.

She wondered what was next....

Coffee?

Tea?

Bed?

"Would you like to watch television?"

She ignored the look in his eyes. He'd known what she was thinking. "That would be nice." She got to her feet, and Nick stood, too.

"You go ahead and I'll be with you shortly. I've got a couple of calls to make first."

She felt a smattering of disappointment, but she quickly pushed it aside. Time alone would let her pulse slow back to its normal beat.

An hour later she was still waiting for Nick to join her. Her favorite sitcom hadn't held her attention, and now a rather boring program was about to start. She could go get her designs and continue working, but she needed a break from them. What's more, she didn't want to interrupt Nick in the study. He could be on an important call.

She yawned.

She felt so tired.

Perhaps she'd just close her eyes for a moment or two.

The next thing she knew a pair of strong masculine arms were lifting her up and carrying her. She tried to clear her mind but she felt warm and protected and she just wanted to snuggle closer.

"Nick?"

"Yes."

It was so hard to open her eyes. "Put me down," she murmured. "I can walk."

"No."

She let out a small sigh. It was too much trouble to argue, especially with her cheek pressed against his chest, his heartbeat beneath it.

He was climbing the stairs now and he smelled so good, his clothes fresh but mixed with his own male scent, his breath retaining a hint of coffee. She'd never been carried by a man before. There was something to be said for all those movies that made it look so romantic being swept off her feet like this.

And then she realized something and she started to giggle. She couldn't help herself.

At the top he paused to look down at her. "What's so funny?"

"You're a little out of breath."

A gleam of amusement twinkled in his eyes. "Are you saying I'm too old to carry you up the stairs?"

"Would I dare?"

"Yes."

All at once she noticed his firm mouth curve up at the corners.

His eyes held a certain glitter. "I'm not too old...or out of breath...to make love to you, my sweet," he murmured, then carried her into their bedroom, kicked the door shut and stood her up against it.

His blue eyes smoldered for her in the lamplight

as he bent his head and kissed her. And he kept right on kissing her until it became a game between them that neither would give up. In the end she had to break away to catch her breath.

He gazed at her triumphantly and before too long he'd stripped the clothes from her body and kissed her again in much more intimate places.

And if he was out of breath by the end of it, he didn't show it. The only thing he showed was a passionate hunger for her that took her by surprise.

Sasha was in the pool when Nick returned early from work the following evening. She'd meant to be showered and changed by now but summer was almost over and she'd wanted to take advantage of the warm weather.

He sat down on the deck chair and loosened his tie, looking handsome but with dark shadows beneath his eyes. She felt guilty for keeping him awake last night, even if it *had* been mutually beneficial.

She trod water in the middle of the pool. "You look tired."

He seemed surprised she'd noticed. "Yeah, I guess I am."

She frowned. "All that driving into the city and back is taking a lot out of you." Commuting to the city took an hour and a half each way, not to mention putting in a full day's work.

He shrugged. "I'll get used to it."

"You shouldn't have to, Nick." She tilted her head at him. "Why don't you get yourself a driver? Your father's had one for many years."

His brow creased in consideration. "Hey, that's not a bad idea. I could hire a permanent driver and that way I can work while I'm in the car and not waste time." He gave her a smile. "Good thinking."

She gave a quick shiver as a late afternoon breeze skipped over her. "Thanks, but I'm sure you would have thought of it yourself."

His gaze dropped to the water lapping at the top of her breasts. "Probably," he said, his distracted tone giving the comment less arrogance.

Her nipples tightened beneath the pink bikini top at the sudden sensual look in his eyes.

He stood up and started undoing his shirt.

"Er...what are you doing?"

"Joining you." He discarded shoes and socks, then his hand went to his belt buckle. Soon he had stripped down to black boxer briefs that fitted him like a second skin, leaving nothing to her imagination.

Her heart thumped erratically. "It's getting a little cold in here."

He gave her a wicked grin. "Then I'll warm you up."

He dove into the pool and she watched him come toward her in the water like a torpedo. The urge to turn and swim for the other side was strong. The temptation to stay and have her defenses annihilated was more exciting.

In one whoosh he came up close to her body and rose to the surface, so close she felt him like a caress. He shook the water from his face and smiled, his wet hair plastered to his head, his sooty lashes spiked with moisture.

"Fancy meeting you here," he drawled, looking what he was: a drop-dead gorgeous male who'd caught the biggest fish in the pool.

Her.

Of course, she was the *only* fish in the pool.

"Yes, fancy that."

The late afternoon sun showed a mischievous gleam in his eye and all at once she knew he was up to something. "Nick," she warned, trying to escape, the water hindering rather than helping.

He laughed playfully and caught her by the waist, before lifting her in the air and tossing her backward. She took a breath just as she went under the water, her mind already on sweet revenge.

She'd get him back, she promised herself as she burst through to the surface. "Nick, you'd—" She gasped. "My bikini top's come off!"

"Really?"

She ignored the relish in his voice and started looking around. Then she saw a pink blob of material near the edge of the pool.

"There it is." She started to swim toward it, aware that Nick was swimming with her. She thought he was merely trying to help her, until they reached it at the same time and he snatched it up and threw it onto the concrete outside of the pool.

"Nick!" She glared at him as she covered her breasts with her hands.

"What?" His eyes danced with the devil.

"How am I going to get out of the pool now?"

"No one's around. Iris is in the kitchen and Leo's gone into Richmond for supplies."

"I'm not a prude but—"

"Yes, you are." He chuckled. "Look at you. I know your body intimately now and yet you're still covering yourself from me."

"You're still a stranger, Nick," she said without thinking.

His smile disappeared. "Am I?" His blue eyes deepened in color. "Then we'd better do something about that."

Without hesitation, he caught her by the waist and pressed her up against the side of the pool.

And then he kissed her.

At first his lips were cold from the water but they soon turned warm enough to have her melting against him. For long, languid moments she reveled in having his mouth take advantage of hers, but eventually he eased back from the kiss.

"Still think of me as a stranger?" he said, a very masculine expression of satisfaction on his face.

A minute ago she'd felt very feminine, but now his words brought her back to reality and she didn't feel in the least like being coquettish. "There's more than knowing a person physically, Nick."

His face closed up. "It'll do for now," he said and turned away. "Stay here. I'll get us some robes."

Sasha watched him heave himself out of the water and stride over to the cabana, all male muscle and sinew. She swallowed hard. What on earth had made her say something so deep like that? Maybe she really *was* a prude and saying that had been her only defense?

He came out wearing a thick white robe and carrying one for her. "I'll cover you as you get out."

Thankful he was still being conscious of her sensitivity, she began climbing up the ladder. It was probably silly to be overreacting but she'd never been one to flaunt her body outrageously and merely because she was no longer a virgin didn't change her way of thinking.

Just as she reached the top of the ladder she looked up in time to see Nick's eyes flicking over her naked breasts. Unable to stop herself, she flushed.

"Put your arms in here," he said huskily, and she did as she was told, feeling more secure once she had the robe cinched in at the waist.

Nick cleared his throat and stepped away from her. "It's still balmy. Would you like to have dinner out here?"

She'd half-expected him to make some excuse to retire to the study. After all, he'd frozen up when she'd started talking about feelings. Fool that she was! The last thing she needed to bring out in the open was any sort of feelings.

To hide her surprise, she pushed back her wet hair. "That would be lovely."

"Good. I'll tell Iris."

"And I'll go dress."

"Let's not bother."

"Er…okay."

He started toward the house, detoured slightly and stopped to pick up something, then came back and handed her the pink bikini top.

Their eyes met and she blushed. "Thanks."

"You're welcome." He turned and walked back toward the house.

She watched him for a moment with her heart thudding, unable to stop herself from admiring those firm legs beneath the bathrobe. She liked the dark hair that was just-so-manly and just-so-touchable and if she dared, when he came back she would love to run her palms up his legs, caressing them, caressing *him*.

All at once she realized she was squeezing her

bikini top. Giving it one last squeeze she dropped it in the pocket of her robe, then went to sit down at the table, her own legs kind of shaky.

And he'd called her a *prude?*

Not any longer.

A few minutes later Nick came back. "Iris will bring out dinner shortly. In the meantime…" He held out two glasses of wine and passed one to her, then went to sit in the chair opposite.

Made selfconscious by her thoughts, she looked away, pretending to concentrate on the guest cottage and glasshouse that could easily been seen from here. Mercifully, the gazebo where they'd shared their kiss was on the other side of the house.

The sound of clinking glass from behind told Sasha that Iris had come out on the patio area. She turned around and smiled as the other woman came toward them pushing a trolley. Before too long she'd left and Sasha and Nick were tucking into their steak and salad.

"How are the designs going?"

She glanced up and saw he'd noticed the paperwork on one of the small tables. She'd been working on them before deciding to take a swim.

"Really well." She hesitated. "Would you like to look over them after dinner?"

"Sure."

After that she turned the conversation to some of the problems she was having with one of the contractors, then they began to talk of the family and other general things.

Nick stood up as soon as they'd both finished eating, and walked over to her designs. Sasha followed him, her heart thumping, wondering if he'd like them. She'd gone to great lengths making sure everything suited the house just right.

"I'm very impressed with these. You've kept the charm of the place without taking too much away from it all."

A swell of relief filled her. "My intention was never to make major changes. I love this place as it is, too, Nick."

His eyes riveted on her face. "Yes, I can see that."

She flushed with pleasure, feeling her cheeks turn almost the same pink as the bikini she wore.

Or *didn't* wear, she mused, pulling the robe tighter over her breasts, seeing his gaze drop to where she pretended she wasn't naked underneath.

"You surprise me," he murmured, lazy seduction seeping into those blue eyes. "I'd have thought you'd put your bikini top back on."

All at once she felt a touch defiant. "Maybe I'm not quite the prude you think I am."

Taking her by surprise, he placed the tip of his finger at her chin. "Hmm, maybe not," he murmured, sending her heartbeat thudding into a mad gallop. Then his finger slithered down her throat to rest on her wildly beating pulse. "You look so damn sexy in that robe."

She moistened her lips. "Nick—"

"I could strip it off you here and now and you wouldn't stop me...would you?"

She was very much afraid he was right.

"And I could slide those tiny bikini bottoms off you and you wouldn't say a word...true?"

Heavens, yes! He could take her this very moment and she'd let him. He made her want to do things she normally didn't do.

How she wished she could lie. "Nick, you know you're right but—"

He dropped his hand away from her throat. "But?"

"Afterwards I would feel totally embarrassed if I thought Iris or Leo had seen us."

His eyes filled with satisfaction. "So you *are* a prude?"

She started to frown. "Are you pleased because I've admitted it? Or because you're right?"

"Both. I like to win."

And he would never give in until he did, she was sure.

Suddenly he said, "I can't help who I am, Sasha."

She looked at him and saw no apology, just a simple statement that made her succumb to her need for him. No, he couldn't help being who he was.

"Nick, please. Take me to bed."

Five

Every evening after that was like a mini-honeymoon for the rest of the week. The weather remained quite warm and Nick would come home and they'd swim in the pool, eat a lazy dinner until dark, then retire to the bedroom.

There Sasha learned she wasn't really a prude at all. She'd just needed to let go of her inhibitions, and with Nick's instructions she did.

And her heart was still intact.

Then one morning she ended up walking past Nick's old bedroom and for some reason she stopped and went in. The room had a large bed and furnishings befitting a teenager of wealth, done out in shades of light and dark brown. On the dresser there were school trophies for cricket, soccer and swimming.

She wasn't sure what she expected to find, but there was something more here, something that made her believe Nick was much deeper than she had previously believed.

She just didn't know what that was.

And perhaps it was best she didn't find out.

Let him be who he was, and leave it at that. She didn't want any more complications in her life.

And speaking of complications, Sasha got a sinking feeling in her stomach when her mother arrived a few hours later right at lunchtime, supposedly to see how things were going. There was nothing for it but to invite her mother to lunch. Not that she minded. It was just that today she seemed to have an agenda.

And Sasha had the feeling it was to do with her father.

"So, you've recovered from the wedding?" Sally asked as they sat down to a light lunch.

"Yes, I have." Until this moment Sasha hadn't let herself be upset that her mother hadn't called since the wedding. *Nick's* mother had managed to call several times.

"I'm sorry I didn't phone you, darling," Sally

said, as if reading her daughter's mind. "I just thought it best I leave you to…adapt."

Sasha gave a remote smile. "Thanks."

"Darling, it's always good to leave a newly married couple to their own devices."

"Is that what the wedding manuals say?" she muttered, then felt bad when she saw the crushed looked on her mother's face. "Mum, I'm sorry. All this has been a bit of a strain. I never expected to get married. Not for a long time anyway."

Sally nodded. "It's okay. I understand. But please remember that you've made your father and me so happy. I love that he's smiling again."

Ignoring the thought that her father probably had a new girlfriend, Sasha squeezed her mother's hand. "Then I'm glad."

Sally's grateful smile turned to a frown. "Darling, there *is* one thing…" she began, making Sasha tense. "There seems to be some sort of delay in closing the deal with Cesare. Your father can't wait much longer, I'm afraid."

"They're pretty busy with the launch in the U.K. and all, I'd imagine."

Come to think of it, she wasn't sure of the reason for the delay herself.

"I was sort of hoping you could ask Nick. Not straight out, mind you. Just see if there's a problem and what it is. I wouldn't ask if it wasn't so important."

Sasha swallowed. "Mum, this is an awkward position you and Dad are putting me in."

Again.

Her mother didn't seem to notice. "Nick's your husband. He'll tell you everything."

There were just so many things a mother could ask a daughter to do. "Nick and I are not in love, Mum. He keeps things to himself. I can't guarantee anything."

"If you could just try, darling."

Sasha sighed. "Okay, I'll see what I can do."

Her mother left straight after the meal, probably in case she said anything to change her daughter's mind. Sasha saw her off with a heavy heart. She loved her mother dearly but she'd never understand her love for a man, which totally submerged her own personality.

That would *never* happen to her.

Never.

And to prove it to herself, she would broach the dreaded subject with Nick at dinner this evening.

"My mother stopped by for lunch today."

Nick looked up from his meal and felt pleased for Sasha's sake. "Good. I don't think you've heard from her since the wedding, have you?"

"She's been busy."

"I'm sure." No doubt looking after Porter's every whim.

And at the expense of her daughter, Nick thought with a frown, surprised at the lack of attention Sally had actually given Sasha since their marriage. Wasn't a mother supposed to fuss over a newlywed daughter? Or was he just being a bit too old-fashioned?

Sasha moistened her mouth. "My mother does have a concern, though. She thought I might be able to help."

"And that is?"

"My father's waiting on a shipping deal to go through with the House of Valente, and apparently it's been delayed. He's not sure why."

Nick leaned back in his chair, and his lips twisted. "And he's sent *his* wife to ask *my* wife why?"

Sasha swallowed, looking uneasy. "He just needs to know, okay? Otherwise he might have to look at other avenues."

"Other avenues?" He almost snorted out loud. Porter was too lazy to go elsewhere when he had Cesare Valente on his side.

"This is business, Nick."

"Exactly."

Her chin angled. "What's that supposed to mean?"

"Stay out of the family business, Sasha."

She gasped. "I thought I *was* part of the family now."

His mouth tightened. "Not the business. That's got nothing to do with you."

"I see." Her green eyes turning cool, she placed her napkin on the table and stood up. "Then perhaps you should have made me sign a prenuptial. Then I won't be able to touch any of your precious family business if we ever divorce." On that note she walked out of the room.

Nick frowned as he watched her leave. They'd only just gotten married, so why the hell was she already mentioning divorce?

Or perhaps she really *had* married him for the money? No, he didn't think that any longer. Why, he couldn't say.

Besides, there was nothing to worry about. No way would she ever get any part of the House of Valente. The legal side of the business was wrapped up tighter than a ball of string.

Dammit, she should stay out of all this anyway. She had her job, and he had his. And what the hell was Porter playing at? The man had no scruples in hiding behind his wife and daughter's skirts. He never had.

It was just a pity the man was so good at detecting trouble. He was obviously suspicious about the delay in signing the contract. And with good reason.

Nick and his brothers couldn't quite put their finger on it, but there was something not quite right about the deal. None of them liked Porter, though this was more than not liking the man. It was a gut feeling that the wool was being pulled over their eyes. But with no real evidence, and unable to share their concerns with Cesare because of his health, they weren't going to be able to postpone the deal much longer.

Damn Porter Blake.

Suddenly Nick realized that Alex should be told the latest development. Yet he didn't want to say any of this on the telephone in case Sasha overheard him and reported back to her father. He grabbed his car keys and left the house.

After that he spent a couple of hours at Alex's place where they talked over the shipping deal once again, trying to find the reason it just didn't feel right. Nothing came to mind, and they reluctantly moved on to the upcoming launch in the U.K.

"Another cup of coffee, Nick?" Olivia asked, sticking her head around the study door.

He smiled at his sister-in-law. "Perhaps one more, Olivia, thanks."

Olivia's gaze slid to Alex. "What about you, honey?"

"No, nothing for me."

Olivia's gaze darted back to Nick, then Alex again, then she smiled oddly and left. Nick knew they were wondering why he wasn't eager to go home to his new wife.

"Problems with Sasha?" Alex said when they were alone again, a speculative look in his eyes.

Nick rubbed the back of his neck. "Just teething problems."

"I understand."

Nick thought about that. "Yes, you do, don't you?"

There was a moment's pause, then Alex said, "Sasha's turned out pretty good, considering what her father's like."

Nick shot him a twisted smile. "Whose side are you on?"

"I'm sure you'll work it out."

Nick suddenly had the urge to go home. So Sasha had only been trying to please her father. He shouldn't have snapped at her like that.

He stood up. "I think I'll give that coffee a miss."

Alex grinned. "I'll tell Olivia."

By the time Nick got home, Sasha was asleep. He showered and slid into bed beside her, careful not to wake her though he was tempted to pull her close. In the end he fell asleep. It had been a long day.

Sasha kept busy the next day going to various stores, but her mind was on Nick and his reaction last night. Stupid hurt had ripped through her at his response. She had hated to ask about the shipping contract but that's all she'd done. It wasn't a major crime. So why was he being so defensive about it?

Of course that threat of hers about a prenuptial had been a childish thing to say, but it served Nick right for drawing such a line in the sand. She already knew he didn't care for her. She hadn't needed to hear that she should stay in the background like a good little wife. It smacked too much of her father.

"You're late."

She almost missed her step as she came through the front door and looked up. Nick was waiting inside and demanding to know where *she'd* been? After he'd left her wondering last night if he'd gone to see an old girlfriend or two.

She placed her handbag on the hall table. "So we're keeping tabs on each other now?"

An odd sincerity flickered across his face. "I was getting worried, that's all."

Her anger cooled. "Okay, if you must know I've been out seeing some contractors. It took longer than I thought it would."

His eyes clouded and all at once he turned toward the living room, his movements somewhat jerky. "Well, I'm glad you're home."

Sasha frowned at his back. Was he embarrassed because he had worried? At the thought, a hint of tenderness trickled through her.

"You could have called me on my cell phone," she suggested quietly, following him into the room.

"I don't know the number."

Her little bubble burst.

"You only had to ask."

"I know."

It said a lot for their relationship.

"Anyway," he continued, "I phoned Iris earlier and told her not to cook dinner. I thought I'd take you out to a local restaurant."

Was this his way of apologizing?

"That would be lovely."

He looked pleased, then, "I'm sorry I snapped at you last night, Sasha. I wanted to apologize when I came home from Alex's, but you were asleep."

So, he'd been at Alex's place. Could she believe that now? Strangely, yes. She just wished she'd known that last night when she'd been upset and pretending to sleep.

"I'm sorry, too," she found herself saying. "I shouldn't have asked. I was worried for my parents' sake, that's all."

"I understand. I should have understood that, too. I—" His cell phone rang. "Damn. I have to take this call."

"Then you do that. I'll go get ready."

He was answering the call even before she'd finished speaking, but Sasha didn't mind. She climbed the stairs, excited now about going out to dinner with her husband.

Thank goodness the wedge between them seemed to have disappeared. She'd hated that her parents had come between them. Hated that Nick had stormed out and left her wondering. And hated it even more when he'd come home and hadn't taken her in his arms.

She was in the shower ten minutes later when the glass door opened and Nick, naked and somewhat aroused, stood there. "Move over, Mrs. Valente."

She didn't need to be told a second time. She willingly moved aside but only a little. Just enough to let him get up close and personal.

Later at the restaurant she and Nick were given a warm welcome by the owner, an Italian man called Angelo.

"I read in the papers that you marry, so tonight I'll cook you both something very special." He beamed at them, then hurried away.

"He seems like a nice man," Sasha said, making small talk as she looked around the restaurant. "You must come here often."

"I used to date his daughter."

"And he's still talking to you?" she joked.

His wry smile conceded the point. "It was very platonic. Angelo knew that."

"He must think highly of you," she said, then pondered the comment while the waiter poured their wine. Italian fathers weren't known for being liberal when it came to their daughters, especially when it came to playboys.

Yet this man had trusted Nick with his daughter? It didn't add up.

When they were alone again, Nick was the first to speak, "So, tell me about living in London. I know you said you lived with your aunt for a while, but you must have liked the place to stay so long."

She was surprised by his sudden interest.

"I loved it. It's such a vibrant city."

His brow arched. "You don't find Sydney vibrant?"

"Yes, but in a different way." She lifted one shoulder. "I guess I was ready to spread my wings and try new adventures."

"You evidently didn't try *too* many new things," he drawled, hinting at her virginity.

She shot him a smile. "I tried enough to keep me happy," she said, then laughed to herself when she saw him frown.

Let him wonder.

Then he said, "Your mother must have missed you."

She felt her smile dim. "I imagine my father did, too."

His eyes shuttered at the mention of her father. "I've been to London quite a few times. I should have stopped in to see you. We could have seen a show together."

"That would have been nice."

She pushed aside the hurt that he hadn't bothered, despite her knowing it was best this way. Having him drop by to see her would have been a painful reminder of the past.

Just then there was a commotion near the front door as people greeted each other with a lot of enthusiasm, giving Sasha the chance to concentrate on something other than the past. Italians really knew how to welcome each other. They were so warm and friendly and—

"Sasha?

She turned back to Nick. "Yes?"

"I said I have a surprise for you."

"A surprise?"

"You'll be happy to know that we'll be signing the contract for your father tomorrow. Now you can tell your mother not to worry."

Intense relief washed over her, then as quickly restrained itself. "Thanks, but I'll wait until it's signed."

His glance sharpened. "You don't trust me?"

"Of course I do."

"Then you don't trust your father."

She hardly dared to breathe. "What makes you say that?"

His eyes narrowed. "I've just realized something. This deal of his was why you changed your mind about marrying me, wasn't it? It wasn't only about merging our two families. Your father wanted to make sure the deal went through, so he forced you to marry me."

Her brain stumbled. Her father would kill her for admitting this, but she couldn't lie.

"He was worried, yes. He thought he might be undercut by a competitor."

"So he made sure he wasn't," Nick said cynically.

Sasha couldn't argue with that. Still, she had to stand up for her father. "I think it's understandable he'd be worried about losing the tender."

Nick's eyes riveted on her, and all at once a mask came down over his face. Perhaps he knew the conversation was leading them places neither of them wanted to go.

He inclined his head. "You're right."

Thankfully Angelo appeared with their meal, and Sasha smiled and praised the food but somehow the evening had been spoiled. Talking about their families always caused friction.

They ate in silence for a while.

"By the way," Nick said eventually. "I've invited a couple of people to dinner Friday night. If you could coordinate it all with Iris that would be great."

All at once she felt a chill. "That's only a couple of days away."

"I know, but they're visiting from Europe and only have Friday night free."

"So it's a business dinner?"

"Yes."

"And you want me to arrange it all and host it as well?"

"Of course."

Her heart sank at his assumption that she would drop everything for him. Not only did she have a late afternoon appointment with one of the contractors, but it reminded her of her parents, her father snapping his fingers and her mother jumping to it.

She'd sworn never to be like her mother.

"You're quiet," Nick said after a few minutes more of silence.

"Am I?"

He looked at her sharply. "What's the matter?"

Her disappointment in him was immense. She should have known not to let herself get close to him again. She would only get hurt a second time.

"You brought me out to dinner to sweeten me up, didn't you?"

His brows drew together. "What are you talking about?"

"Actually I'm surprised you even did that," she scoffed. "Did you think I would say no, Nick? Well, you're right. I *am* saying no."

His face hardened. "No to what?"

"To arranging your business dinner and playing your hostess."

"You're my wife."

She bristled. "Yes, not your slave to be told what to do and when to do it."

He sat back, his eyes assessing hers. "Where's all this coming from?"

"I'm sick of being expected to drop everything for everyone else. First my parents expect me to give up my freedom for them, and now you think I should just fall in with whatever plans you make."

And truth to tell, she was sick of being a nobody to Nick. Because that's what it all came down to. He hadn't been interested in her years ago. He still wasn't interested in her.

Not as a person.

A pulse began to beat in his cheekbone. "I didn't mean to treat you like your father does."

She gave a silent gasp. Clearly he thought of her as her father's lackey as well. "Thanks very much."

"You know what I mean."

Hurt gnawed at her. "Unfortunately, yes, I do."

His gaze rested on her face with a hint of regret. "Sasha, I'm sorry. I'll take them to a restaurant in the city. You don't need to come."

She sighed, suddenly feeling bad yet knowing she shouldn't. "Nick, if you were to *ask* me, then I don't mind hosting the dinner. I just don't like the expectation that I have to do it."

He considered her across the table. "Then would

you mind being my hostess on Friday, Sasha? I'd really appreciate it."

Her heart thudded at the sincerity in his tone. "Yes. I'm happy to help." She would reschedule her appointment with the contractor.

His shoulders relaxed a little, and there was an odd amusement in his eyes. "You're quite fiery when you're upset. I never noticed that when you were growing up. You were always quite shy."

Shy and in love.

Her stomach did a flip at the thought. "Perhaps I didn't want you to notice back then," she lied.

"And now?"

She took a moment to answer as past hurts rose in her throat. "I'm older. I want respect."

"You always had my respect, Sasha."

"No, Nick. I didn't."

He went still, his eyes probing hers. "Then I'm sorry if I made you feel that way. It wasn't intentional."

"I know." And therein lay the crux of the matter. It was another example of her meaning less than nothing to him.

Angelo reappeared to check that their meal was enjoyable and Sasha welcomed the interruption. She'd said more than enough. If Nick didn't think she mattered, then she wasn't going to force him to change his mind.

She had her pride after all.

Six

Nick phoned Sasha late the following morning to tell her the deal had been signed and that Alex was calling her father now to tell him the news.

Enormously relieved, Sasha thanked him for letting her know, then waited for her mother to call and share in the good news and perhaps say thanks.

Her mother didn't call.

"No doubt your parents were relieved," Nick said when he came home.

"No doubt they were."

He froze. "You mean they haven't called you?"

A lump lodged in her throat. "No, but they were probably busy."

"They weren't too busy to ask you to spy for them," he rasped.

She sucked in a sharp breath. "It wasn't like that."

A pulse beat in his cheekbone. "Not on your part, but they got what they wanted from you. They used you, Sasha."

He was right, and on one level she was warmed by his concern for her, but loyalty to her mother kept her quiet. "Let's forget that for now."

"Can you?"

"No." If she thought about it the pain would overwhelm her. She'd always known she came second with her mother, but until recently she hadn't realized just how low down on the scale she was compared with her father.

She pretended to dismiss it all. "Come on. I want you to pick a color scheme for the study. I can't decide by myself."

He made a dismissive gesture. "Any color will do."

"No, Nick. You'll be using it a lot, so it's important I get your input."

"You'll be using it, too."

"Exactly. It's something we need to choose together."

He suddenly broke into a sexy half smile. "You're very good at getting your own way. Subtle but very effective."

She found herself smiling back. "That's always been my policy."

The rest of the week went quickly and before she knew it, it was Friday. She was nervous about hosting their first dinner, and of course she helped Iris arrange it all, but there was a difference in doing it because she wanted to and not because it was expected of her.

"You look beautiful," Nick said when she'd finished dressing in a blue dress that hugged her body in all the right places, her blonde hair up in a chignon, delicate diamond earrings at her ears.

Silly delight rippled through her. "Thanks." Her eyes slid over his dark suit and white shirt that did him full-on justice. "You're looking quite spiffy yourself."

He smiled. "Spiffy, eh?"

She smiled back then saw him fiddling with his tie. "Here, let me do that for you."

"You don't mind?"

"No, I like doing up men's ties," she quipped as she stepped close to him and began working on the tie.

His smile vanished. "Just how many men's ties have you done up?"

"The odd one or two."

He stared down at her, then must have seen her lips twitching because he broke into a grin. "I think you're making that up."

"Am I?"

"You'd better be," he pretended to growl, sending a thought flashing through her mind. He *liked* being the only man to make love to her.

Well, well, she mused. Who'd have thought he'd be so old-fashioned?

"You're not nervous about tonight?" he asked, dragging her from her thoughts.

"Yes, I am."

"You don't show it."

"Neither do you."

One brow rose. "Who said I was nervous?"

"You usually don't have trouble doing up your tie."

"Thanks for noticing," he said wryly.

She finished her task and patted the tie. "There. That's better."

He turned away to look in the mirror. "Perfect."

Yes.

He was.

She cleared her throat. "So this dinner is important, is it?"

He reached for his jacket. "Yes and no. Alex has already made the deals to launch 'Valente's Woman' in France and Germany. I just need to keep relations agreeable between us until the launch."

Sasha realized that this must be all quite new to Nick. Previously Cesare and Isabel would have hosted any clients, and then Alex and Olivia, but this time it fell to him. No doubt he would be an accomplished host as a playboy bachelor, but this was the first time he'd be hosting a dinner in his own home as a married man.

She felt bad now for refusing before. "You'll do fine," she said, prompting an arrogant smile from him.

"I know."

And he did.

Extra fine, Sasha thought sourly an hour later as she watched Claudine, the beautiful wife of the French businessman, flirt with Nick from the moment she set foot in the house.

In the meantime the German couple just sat back and smiled, along with Jacque, who didn't appear concerned by his wife's behavior.

It concerned Sasha, especially when Nick looked thoroughly smitten by the gorgeous brunette leaning close to him and talking French in a low, husky voice.

"Ooh, Nicolah, you are teasing me," she said in her accented English, laughing sexily as she squirmed in her seat.

"No, really," he teased. "If you're going to the fashion show tomorrow make sure they don't mistake you for one of their models."

Claudine preened. "Perhaps I will need you to

come with me and protect me." She looked at Sasha. "Would you mind if I borrowed your husband tomorrow, Sasha?"

Her blatant approach took Sasha's breath away. And Nick, the rat, was sitting there smiling and thoroughly enjoying himself and probably expected she would say yes.

She'd be damned if she'd be humiliated like this.

"I'm sorry, Claudine, but I need him tomorrow," she said sweetly, smiling at Nick like her very existence depended on him.

"Ooh," Claudine pouted at Nick. "Another time perhaps, Nicolah?"

"It's a date."

Sasha could feel the humiliation rise up in her throat but she refused to look at the others at the table. A date with a married woman? Wasn't he forgetting something? Like he was now a married man himself? This was going beyond being more than a good host.

Or perhaps he just didn't care. Perhaps he was too focused on making a conquest to worry about what this meeting was all about. Worse, perhaps this was how he did business as a playboy.

A reputation well earned?

Thankfully the German woman, Freda, asked Sasha about her plans to redecorate and the conversation turned to interior design. She was busy answering questions when she heard Claudine ask Nick if he could show her where she could freshen up.

"That's okay, Claudine," she said instantly. "I can show you."

"Oh but…you are talking to Freda."

"No, that's fine. I want to freshen up, too."

The woman pouted again, but Sasha ignored it, just as she ignored Nick as she passed him on her way out the door. If he dared to chastise her later, then he was in for a rude shock.

"Your name is French?" Claudine asked as they walked down the hallway. It was the first personal thing she'd said to her all night.

"No. It's spelled S-A-S-H-A, not S-A-C-H-A."

"You are not French then?"

"No."

Claudine gave a grunt, evidently not impressed by a non-French person using a French-sounding name.

Then the woman sent her a sideways glance. "Nicolah is so handsome."

Aah, now they were getting to the main thing.

Sasha just smiled. "Very."

And he's mine, she wanted to say.

"Jacques does not like the fashion shows." She sighed deeply. "It's a pity Nicolah cannot come with me. I'm sure he would like that."

Sasha opened the bathroom door. "Family always comes first with Nick."

And as she shut the door behind the woman, Sasha realized that was the truth. His family did always come first.

Just not his wife.

Nick was glad to see the back of their guests. Now all he wanted to do was go to bed—with Sasha.

"That went well," he said, coming into the bedroom after he'd turned off most of the downstairs lights. Sasha was sitting in front of the dressing table, taking off her jewelry. She looked so right, so very feminine, and for the first time he felt thoroughly married.

It wasn't a bad feeling.

"For some," she said coolly.

Her unfriendly tone dragged him from his pleasant thoughts. "What do you mean?"

She spun around on the stool, and suddenly sparks were flying from her green eyes. "I'm sorry if I spoiled your plans for tomorrow, Nick, but I didn't think it right you go out on a *date* with another woman when you're already married to me."

He stared in amazement, then snorted. "You didn't think that was for real, did you? Claudine was just flirting."

And mild flirting at best. He'd known women who came on a lot stronger than that.

"Is that why she was practically begging me to let you go to the fashion show with her?"

"When?"

"When I escorted her to the bathroom."

He shrugged. "She's French. She does things over the top."

"Not with *my* husband she doesn't."

A crazy thought blew him away. "You're jealous!"

Her slim shoulders tensed. "Don't be ridiculous. You promised to be faithful, and I expect you to keep that promise, that's all."

Okay, so she wasn't jealous.

And now he was getting annoyed. His word was good enough for the rest of the world. It should be good enough for his wife.

"Look, I told you I take my marriage vows seriously, and I do. There's no way I'll be unfaithful to you."

"I'm trying to believe that."

He considered her tight mouth. "You've really got a thing about this, haven't you?"

She hesitated, then, "Yes, I do. I've spent a lifetime watching my father having affair after affair and my poor mother putting up with it. Not me. I won't put up with it. I won't allow myself to be humiliated in such a way."

The words were heartfelt, and something kicked inside him. "So you know about your father's affairs?"

"Doesn't everyone?" she said with a catch in her voice.

"Does your mother know?"

"We've never mentioned it, but I'm sure she does." She straightened her shoulders. "And I won't ever let myself be put in that position."

"I'm not asking you to."

Her expression clouded. "It's all about respect, isn't it?" she said, as if talking to herself. "Respect for another person."

"You've got my respect."

She focused back on him. "But I didn't always have it, did I?"

The muscles at the back of his neck tightened. She'd mentioned respect the other day, too, and he'd let the comment pass. Not this time.

"Why do you say that? I've always treated you with respect."

"If you'd respected me years ago you wouldn't have gone off with that girl after our kiss."

The comment staggered him. "What are you saying? That our kiss *mattered* to you back then?"

She held his gaze for a moment, and her delicate chin rose higher. "You gave me my first kiss, Nick. And yes, it mattered."

He expelled a breath.

"But you didn't care, Nick."

She was wrong about that.

"You've got no idea how hard it was for me to walk away from you, Sasha. But dammit, you were only eighteen. You had your whole life ahead of you."

"So did you."

"I don't deny that. I was only twenty-five. I didn't want a serious relationship. It wouldn't have been fair to you—to either of us—if I'd taken what you'd offered."

"I felt humiliated," she said quietly. "More so when you left with another girl."

He swore low in his throat. "I'm sorry. That hadn't been my intention."

He'd gotten the hell out of there with the other girl—he couldn't even remember her name now—not to humiliate but because Sasha was a siren...a little witch...who'd suddenly developed a body and a face to die for.

Knowing himself, he would have taken what was offered and moved on.

Knowing Sasha, he couldn't have done that to her.

She gave a shaky sigh. "That was the worst part. You had no idea how devastated I was."

His heart jolted inside his chest. Had this been more than Sasha testing out her newfound womanly ways?

"Sasha, did you have a crush on me?"

For a moment their eyes locked.

"Yes, Nick. I did. I was a young girl in love with the man of her dreams."

Oh hell.

Dare he ask....

"Are you still in love with me, Sasha?"

Her eyelids flickered. "I'm fond of you, Nick, but that's all." As if the thought didn't deserve any further comment, she spun on her stool to face the mirror again and began brushing her hair.

It was odd but his stomach felt like it had just been hollowed out. She hadn't missed a beat in her answer. Love definitely wasn't in her agenda.

Not that he would have known what to do if she *had* said she loved him. He hadn't figured on *that* in their plans. He'd be happy with fondness between them.

And desire.

That was enough.

He walked up behind her and put his hands on her shoulders, looking at her through her reflection. "Amazing as it may seem to you, you're the only woman I want in my life right now."

And that was the truth.

The brush stilled in her hand. "I...I am?"

Her stutter was charming and made his heart pound against his ribs. She may not be in love with him, but she was so very beautiful.

"Yes," he murmured, sliding the neckline of her dress aside and kissing her bare shoulder. "Let me show you."

* * *

At breakfast, Sasha was still recovering from Nick's questions last night.

Are you still in love with me, Sasha?

No, she wasn't, but the question had made her uncomfortable. Love wasn't an easy subject to discuss at any time, but talking about it made it seem more real, even possible.

It was a possibility she didn't want.

Just then, Iris opened the door to the breakfast room and Cesare and Isabel came walking in.

Nick put down his napkin in surprise. "Dad, what are you doing here?"

Cesare's step seemed to hesitate. "Son, I have something to tell you."

Sasha saw Nick stiffen.

"What's happened, Dad?"

Cesare sat down on one of the chairs, his face paler than usual. At the same time, Isabel hugged Nick, then straightened but kept her hand on his shoulder in a comforting gesture. Sasha swallowed hard. This was definitely bad news.

"It's your mother, *figlio mio*." The older man paused. "She fell asleep at the wheel of her car last night and crashed into a parked truck."

Sasha gasped.

Nick sat like stone. "And?"

"She's dead, Nick. She died instantly."

Pain for Nick squeezed Sasha's heart as Isabel squeezed his shoulder.

Nick didn't move. "Had she been drinking?"

"We don't know. Perhaps."

Nick's lips twisted. "More than likely she was coming home from a party."

Cesare inclined his head. "She lived life on her terms, Nick."

"You don't have to tell me that, Dad," Nick said, jumping to his feet and going over to the patio door. He stood looking out over the sunny courtyard.

"At least she didn't suffer, honey," Isabel murmured. "None of us would want that."

Nick let out a deep sigh but didn't turn around. "No, I wouldn't have wanted that."

Seconds passed without anyone speaking as if in deference to the dead.

"They're arranging the funeral for Tuesday in Melbourne," Cesare finally said.

"I won't be going."

Cesare's mouth clamped in a thin line. "She was your mother, son."

"Really?" Nick turned around to face them, the lines of his face rigid.

"I know how you feel, but the world is made up of different people. We have to accept that."

"*You* accept it." Nick tilted his head. "Actually, you accepted that years ago, didn't you?"

Cesare stiffened. "Your mother wasn't the woman I thought she was when I married her, I know. But I did learn to accept that's how she was."

"I'm sorry, but I can't be so generous."

Cesare's gaze held his son's. "The best thing that came out of our marriage was *you*, Nick."

Sasha's throat thickened.

A muscle ticked in Nick's cheek. "Emotional blackmail won't work this time, Dad. I won't go to the funeral. I don't owe her anything."

Cesare was having none of that. He straightened his shoulders. "Julieann was a Valente, if even for a short while. She should have someone from the Valente family go to the funeral."

"You go then."

Cesare glanced at Isabel then back. "I can't. I would if I could, but—"

"His doctor won't let him go," Isabel said. "He's worried it will be too much for your father."

Cesare made a dismissive gesture. "The doctor's just being too cautious. He thinks you'll sue him if I die."

Isabel tutted. "Now, you know that's not true, Cesare." She looked at Nick. "For what it's worth I don't think you should be forced to go either."

"Thanks for your support, Izzie," Cesare muttered.

She looked at her husband. "I don't care what you

say. I don't think anyone should have to go if they don't want to, Cesare."

For some reason, Sasha thought of her own father and how she'd feel if he'd walked out on them years ago. Would she have been forgiving of him?

Probably not.

Of course, it may have turned out better if her father *had* left them. Her mother may have had a chance at a decent life.

"I'm not going, Dad."

Cesare got to his feet, his mouth firming with purpose. "Then it's up to me." He shot Isabel a look. "And no more about it from you, my darling wife. I—" Suddenly he turned pale.

"Dad?" Nick raced over while Isabel gasped, then took some tablets out of Cesare's jacket pocket.

"Here, darling. Put this under your tongue."

A short while later Cesare started to get his color back and everyone breathed a sigh of relief. If the older man had been hoping for effect, he couldn't have chosen a better moment.

Nick stood looking down at his father, his eyes unreadable. "Okay, Dad. You get your wish. I'll go to the funeral."

Cesare looked relieved. "Thank you, *figlio mio*. This means a lot to me."

"I'll go with him," Sasha said, wanting them to know she'd be there for Nick.

Nick spun toward her. "No."

"But—"

"No." Without another word, he turned and walked out of the room.

Sasha's heart sank, but she wasn't about to give up.

"Go with him, honey," Isabel said. "He needs you."

Sasha nodded. He needed someone, but she wasn't sure it was her. "I intend to, Isabel. Don't worry."

After that, the older couple left and Sasha saw them off. For all that she understood why Cesare wanted a Valente at the funeral, like Isabel, she did think it unfair to ask Nick to go. Did they really need someone to represent the family? Wasn't Cesare showing the woman more compassion than she'd shown him and their son?

But it wasn't her place to say anything.

She knocked on the study door and went in. "Nick—"

"No, Sasha."

"But—"

"I'm going alone."

She stopped in the middle of the room and glared at him across the desk. "Would you let me finish a sentence or are you taking a page from my father's book now?"

He flinched.

"Nick, look. I know we were forced to get married, and I know we didn't marry for love, but I...care about you. I'm your wife, and I should go with you at a time like this."

A nerve pulsed near Nick's temple. "It's a funeral for a woman you didn't even know, Sasha. There's no reason for you to attend."

"I may not have known the woman, but I know her son very well. *He's* reason enough for me to go."

His eyes darkened as silence hung in the air. She meant every word. She wouldn't back down over this.

Something shifted in his expression as he looked at her. Finally he said, "As you wish."

Her heart thudded with relief. "Thank you."

He picked up the phone. "Now, if you don't mind, I have some arrangements to make." Clearly he wanted to push her out, both of the room and emotionally.

Still, she hung on. "Would you like me to do all that?"

"Thanks, but my PA knows my requirements."

She inclined her head and went to leave the room. It was obvious he'd given all he had to give right now.

"Sasha?"

She stopped and turned. "Yes?"

"Thank you," he said brusquely.

She nodded and shut the door behind her, not

sure what he was thanking her for—wanting to go
to the funeral with him, or offering to help. Her heart
swelled inside her chest. Nick really did appreciate
her efforts.

He had finally noticed.

Seven

With Alex using the family jet in England, making it unavailable to take to Melbourne, Nick was glad he'd hired another plane. At least this way he wouldn't leave the tainted memories of the funeral in the family jet and could put it all behind him once it was over.

He only wished Sasha had stayed at home, he thought, watching her in the leather chair opposite as she stared out the aircraft window. She was dressed appropriately in black and looked elegantly sedate, but he still didn't think this funeral was the place for her. He appreciated her concern, but it wasn't warranted. He could handle this by himself.

Dammit, his mother didn't deserve to have Valente representation at her funeral. Okay, so his father had wanted to do the right thing, but then, his father had always wanted to do the right thing. The older man just hadn't known there had been a price to pay.

And that *he'd* been the one to pay it.

An hour later they pulled up outside the church and a knot tightened in Nick's gut. Just as he squared his shoulders he heard Sasha gasp.

"It's beautiful," she murmured, looking up at the church through the limousine window.

He took a glance but he wasn't really interested in a building right now.

She sat back on the seat and winced. "Oh, Nick, I'm sorry. This isn't the right time to say that."

"It's fine."

She shook her head. "No, I was being insensitive. It's just that this is the type of church I always dreamed I'd be married in."

That caught his attention. "You did?"

She flushed, then gave a shrug. "Sorry. It took me by surprise when I saw it."

Just like she was taking him by surprise.

"No need to apologize," he said, as the driver opened the car door.

Nick had the strangest feeling when he saw his mother's casket near the altar. He stopped inside the door, his legs unable to move. This was his *mother,* something inside him screamed.

And then he felt Sasha touch his arm and at that moment he was truly grateful to have her with him.

The service was brief with only about twenty people who'd bothered to come. Two of the men he remembered as her husbands from years ago. Not much for a life spent with five husbands and various lovers.

A life spent on the edge.

Outside the church a man in his early sixties came up to him and shook his hand. "Nick, she would have been so happy you came."

Nick's brows flattened. "And you are?"

"I was Julieann's husband."

"Husband?" Nick bit back from asking which one.

"Her last one," the man said, reading his mind. "My name's Ted, by the way."

Ted's eyes darted to Sasha. "And this must be your new wife," he said, startling Nick, then explained, "Julieann read about your marriage in the papers."

Nick grimaced inwardly. He wondered how long before his mother would have found a way to make use of that knowledge.

"How long were you married, Ted?"

"Five years." The older man's eyes didn't waver. "She'd changed, Nick."

"Really? So she wasn't drunk behind the wheel of her car when she died?"

"No, she wasn't," Ted said firmly. "She'd been working the nightshift at an old people's home. She fell asleep because she was tired."

"My mother would never have been working. Period. And certainly not working to help anyone else."

Ted began to look upset. "I told you, she'd changed. Believe me, she had."

Nick held himself in check. Nothing would convince him of that statement. "It doesn't matter if I believe you or not. It's over."

The older man blinked rapidly, then reached into his pocket and pulled out an envelope. "I think you should have this."

Nick didn't take it. "What is it?"

"It's a letter. To you. She was planning on sending it, but kept putting it off until she felt you were ready."

Nick still didn't take it. "I don't want it. It's too late."

Ted continued to hold out the envelope but his hand shook a little now. "Then it won't do any harm for you to read it."

Nick stared hard at him. "Were you good to my mother, Ted?"

Moisture refilled Ted's eyes as he straightened. "Yes, I was."

"Then I'll take it for your sake." Nick took the envelope, aware of the other man's relief. He couldn't promise to ever read it. "I'm sorry for your loss, Ted."

"I'm sorry for yours, too, son."

Swallowing a lump in his throat, Nick cupped Sasha's elbow and walked her to the limousine. Ted had no need to offer condolences for losing his mother.

You couldn't lose something you had never had.

After dinner that evening, Sasha wasn't surprised when Nick said he was going to do some work in the upstairs study. He'd already spoken to his father about the funeral, and then Alex had called from London with concern in his voice.

She knew Nick was upset and he needed to be alone to think about the day's events. She understood he was having trouble assimilating what Ted had told him about his mother, how to fit that image into the person Nick knew her to be. She could only imagine the thoughts going through his head right now.

Of course, he hadn't needed to hear her exclaim over the church like they were attending a joyous wedding instead of a solemn funeral. Yet she hadn't been able to stop herself. The moment she'd seen it, she'd fallen in love with its picture-book setting. The perfect picture for the perfect wedding she had dreamed about.

She sighed and pushed aside her wistful thoughts as she settled down to do some work of her own. For once, time dragged. She wanted to go and see how Nick was doing.

For a few hours she held back, but at nine o'clock she couldn't wait any longer. She went upstairs and knocked on the study door, only to find him nowhere to be seen.

And then she saw the letter from his mother lying open on the desk. Her heart started to thud.

Hurrying to the window she saw his car was still parked outside in the driveway. Then she checked their bedroom but he wasn't there either. She was about to go downstairs and check the kitchen when she noticed a door open at the far end of the landing.

Nick's old bedroom.

She found him sitting on the side of the bed in the dark, the light from the hallway spilling across the center of the room, showing him with his elbows on his knees, staring down at the floor.

"Nick?" she murmured with concern, wanting to rush to him but not wanting to intrude in a private moment.

He lifted his head. "Sasha."

"Are you okay?"

A moment's silence, then he straightened. "Yeah, I am."

She took a few steps into the room. "I went to look

for you in the study." She hesitated. "Um...I saw your mother's letter was open and I was concerned for you."

"Did you read it?"

"No! I would never do that."

He grimaced. "I wasn't accusing. I thought you might have read it to see if it had upset me, that's all."

"And has it? Upset you, that is."

"Yes and no." He took a ragged breath. "No, because my mother truly was genuinely sorry for all she'd done. Yes, because it's too late to tell her I forgive her."

Stunned surprise rippled through her and she sat down on one of the brocade chairs. "You forgive her?"

He nodded. "My mother was never the type of person to ask for forgiveness. You see, she never actually realized she needed forgiving in the first place." He gave a half smile at that. "And I would've said a leopard never changed its spots, but some things happened to Julieann that had a profound effect on her."

"What was that?"

"She fell in love for the first time ever. With Ted." He gave a tiny pause. "And she got cancer."

Sasha's heart saddened for the woman. "Cancer?"

"Yes, and she recovered but it made her look back on her life and see all the hurt she'd caused. Believe me, I know the woman my mother was in her younger years, and she would never have written that letter. Never."

Sasha knew he would never let himself be fooled by anything insincere. "I'm glad she changed for the better."

"Me, too." Then his brows pulled together. "I guess for once my father was right and I was wrong. If Dad hadn't convinced me to go, I'd probably have received the letter in the mail and not read it at all. I know for sure I wouldn't have been so quick to forgive, but meeting Ted today convinced me he was genuine. And that the letter was, too."

"I liked Ted."

"Me, too. He's much better than her previous husbands. There were five," he said before she could ask. "And apart from Ted, they were all after my mother for the money she could get out of my father."

Sasha's forehead creased. "Did your father just hand over money whenever she asked for it?"

He shook his head. "No, it wasn't quite like that. From the time I was seven she'd turn up here every couple of years until I was twelve, and insist on my staying with her and her current husband for a few days while they were in town." His lips twisted. "Naturally she'd insist on being paid 'expenses' and then blow it all at the races."

Sasha listened with rising dismay. She was beginning to see why Nick had disliked his mother so much.

"My dad didn't want to stop me from seeing her, but he would always ask me if I wanted to go. I thought he wanted me to, so I did." He shrugged. "I've never told him the truth."

Her eyebrows rose. "Your father didn't realize this? He just handed you over to a woman who had no respect for anyone or took no responsibility for anything?"

"He thought he was doing the right thing. Besides, he told me years later he had someone keep an eye on me while I was away, and he thought I was having an okay time. She'd dump me on her parents, you see, while they went off to the races, so he thought I was getting to know my grandparents. They couldn't have been less interested in me if they'd tried."

Oh, poor Nick. "What did you do when you were with them?"

"Sit and watch television. I was miserable and couldn't wait to get back home." He took a shuddering breath. "It was only a few days, but it felt like a lifetime."

"And there would've always been the fear that you would never come back home again," she said half to herself.

A muscle began to throb in his cheek.

She stared aghast. "Oh my God. That's why you won't let me redecorate this bedroom. This was your sanctuary whenever you returned home, wasn't it?"

He nodded with a taut jerk of his head. "Yes. I felt safe here. I still do. I used to imagine they would never get to me here."

Her heart constricted. "Oh, Nick. I'm sorry you had to go through all that."

"Hey, it wasn't so bad," he said, making light of it now.

"Yes, it was."

A look of discomfort crossed his face. "Okay, so those times were bad, but I always made it back home and that's the important thing."

She looked at Nick and something tumbled around in her chest. She could imagine him a little boy or a young teenager putting on a brave face, terrified of going with his mother and her latest new husband, not knowing if he would ever come back to those who loved him.

The urge to hold him was strong and she stood up and went to stand between his legs, pulling his head against her breast in a comforting fashion. He didn't resist, and they remained like that for a while.

Only, suddenly, she wanted more tonight. She wanted to show him that this was their home and she was his wife and he had no need to fear being abandoned ever again.

She turned his head up to her. "Let me make love to you, Nick."

His eyes flared with desire. "Yes, Sasha," he said in a low, raspy voice. "I need you to love me tonight."

His words cut the air from her lungs.

Love him?

Oh God, she thought as she bent her head and began placing soft kisses down his cheek until she came to his mouth.

She already did.

Eight

The next morning Sasha felt Nick's lips on hers in a brief goodbye kiss, but she kept her eyes shut until she heard him leave the room. Then and only then did she carefully open them to a new morning and a new beginning, one where she knew she would have to be strong.

She loved him.

If it hadn't been for all the smoke and mirrors caused by their forced marriage she'd probably have seen it coming. As it was, it had taken a private man like Nick to share his painful past with her to make her see what was truly in her heart.

She'd never stopped loving him.

She'd merely been convincing herself otherwise because it hurt too much to admit she loved a man who would never love her back. He couldn't. He wasn't the type of man to give up part of himself for love of a woman. Even now, she knew he didn't love her. He liked her, and she was sure he liked her even more with each passing day, but there was no way she could tell him she loved him.

He wouldn't want to know.

And his rejection of her would be far worse this time. They were adults now and their feelings ran deeper and more lasting, and to bring it out in the open would ruin any chance of a happy marriage between them.

A marriage now based on friendship.

Not love.

No, she'd have to be happy with what she had. The alternative of a divorce, or of Nick feeling uncomfortable around her was too much to bear.

Better to keep it a secret.

Of course, for all her self-talk, when he returned home that night and kissed her hello, then took the stairs two at a time to go shower and change, Sasha's heart skipped a beat as she realized something. This morning's kiss before leaving for work had been the first time he'd kissed her goodbye.

And now this?

Things had definitely changed for the better between them. Perhaps one day...

No, she dared not think it.

"By the way," he said over dinner later. "I'm happy for you to redecorate my old bedroom now."

She blinked. "You are?"

"Yes. Give it a whole new look and turn it into a spare bedroom. Do whatever you want. You're the expert. I don't need it anymore."

Her insides turned soft. "No, you don't, do you?"

He seemed much more relaxed. "Sasha, I think it's time we had some fun. Would you like to go to a party on Saturday night? Friends of mine are celebrating their fifth wedding anniversary."

She liked that he was asking her and not merely expecting her to go. More importantly it was as if he actually *wanted* to be with her.

"I'd love to go to the party with you."

He flashed her a smile. "Good."

That smile made her senses spin and took her right through the week, especially when he continued to kiss her goodbye and hello every day. It was as if he truly considered her his real wife now.

There were about fifty people at the party held at a gorgeous mansion overlooking the Parramatta River. Nick's friends, Fiona and Boyd, were warm and friendly.

"We're so sorry we missed your wedding," Fiona said. "We were overseas at the time but it was a nice surprise when we came back."

"Surprise?" Boyd laughingly choked. "I was totally shocked when Nick told me he was married. Who'd have thought the playboy would ever get married, let alone so quickly?" He got an elbow in the ribs by his wife. "I mean…well, you know what I mean."

"Yeah, Boyd, we know what you mean," Nick teased and left it at that.

Sasha was grateful Nick didn't tell them the truth. She hadn't cared at the wedding if everyone had known, but now it was a matter of pride.

And a matter of love.

Over the next hour Nick kept her by his side, not leaving her for a minute while they mixed with a small group of friends. They were laughing at something one of the wives said when suddenly a blonde beauty pushed through the group.

"Darling!" she squealed, throwing her arms around Nick's neck and hugging him. She leaned back and kissed him full on the mouth before saying, "Darling, I'm back. Aren't you glad to see me?"

There was dead silence in the group.

Sasha swallowed hard as she looked at the beautiful blonde, then Nick, seeing the shock before a mask came down over his face.

Effortlessly he extricated himself from the

woman's arms and slid his arm around Sasha's waist and said, "Brenda, I'd like you to meet my wife."

The other woman gasped, her eyes darting in disbelief to Sasha and back. "Your *wife?*"

"That's what I said."

The blonde's face began to crumble. "Oh, Nick, how could you!" she choked, spinning on her heels and racing out to the patio.

The silence continued.

Nick's mouth tightened as he turned to Sasha. "I'd better go sort this out."

Sasha nodded. It was the right thing to do, the only decent thing to do, so why was she feeling uneasy about it all? He strode away, leaving an uncomfortable quiet.

Then Fiona took matters into hand. "These things happen," she said sympathetically, giving Sasha's arm a pat.

Sasha cleared her throat. "Yes, they do."

Then one of the men started talking about something else and the conversation started up again somewhat awkwardly, everyone no doubt wondering what was going on out there on the patio and none more than herself.

She held her head high and determined to keep on doing so, but inside she was feeling less than certain. Who was Brenda, and how much had she and Nick meant to each other?

It seemed forever before he returned. His jaw was clenched as he came up and slipped his arm around her waist again, pulling her close. "Right, I'm back where I belong now."

She knew he meant to comfort her but their relationship was such that she didn't know which way the wind would blow. All this could be for show.

She winced. What was the matter with her? It *was* all for show.

All at once Brenda appeared at the open doorway, tears streaming down her beautiful face as she gave a loud sob and ran through the room to the front door. Every pair of eyes watched her, then all those eyes seemed to turn and look at her and Nick.

Sasha wanted to sink through the floor.

"Let's dance," he rasped, taking her drink and handing it to Boyd. Then he led her toward an area set aside for dancing.

He pulled her into his arms. "Don't ask."

"Nick, I—"

"Later. Right now I want to dance with my wife."

She kept quiet but as she looked into his angry blue eyes she had to wonder if there was a reason he had called her his wife.

Was it to remind her that he was married to her?

Or was it a reminder to himself?

Thankfully by the time they'd finished their

dance, the commotion Brenda had caused had receded into the background. Everyone had gone back to enjoying themselves and she was touched that some of the ladies seemed to be going out of their way to be nice to her.

She just hoped it wasn't from pity. She couldn't bear that. Not when she'd seen so many others pity her mother over the years.

They stayed at the party for an hour after that, more out of pride than not, Sasha knew. Once in the car, she couldn't hold back any longer. She had to know.

"Do you love her?"

Nick's hand stilled on the ignition key. "Of course not."

"She loves you."

His mouth tightened as he lowered his hand. "She thinks she does. She'll get over it."

Just like *she* had got over him years ago?

Just like *she* would have to get over her love for him now?

"That's so hard-hearted, Nick."

"What do you want me to say, Sasha? I'm married now. I can't help her."

Pain wrapped around her heart. "Would you help her if you *weren't* married?"

He shot her a hard glance. "No."

Is that all he had to say?

"Look, she went overseas and married someone else, and now she's walked out on that marriage after six months and is pretending she still wants me? No way."

She swallowed hard. Couldn't he see what was right in front of him?

"Maybe she really does love you."

He made a harsh sound. "Sure. Brenda came back through that room knowing everyone would feel sorry for her. Don't you think a truly broken-hearted person would leave by the back door and away from prying eyes? Does all that sound like love to you?"

Her heart began to fill with relief. "No, I guess it doesn't."

"I was the one who broke it off. Brenda was a fling, that's all. I would never have married her."

"Never?"

"Never." He reached out and put his hand over hers. "I'm glad I'm married to you."

She ignored the warmth of his skin against her own. "Why?"

He blinked. "Why?"

"That's what I said."

Withdrawal came over his face before he turned back to put the key in the ignition. "There's a whole heap of reasons."

Yes, and none of them were love.

He glanced back at her. "Sasha, don't let her get to you. She's someone from my past and I can't change that. But don't let her into our future, okay?"

He was right.

"Okay."

He waited a moment more, his eyes reading hers as if to be convinced, then he started up the engine and headed for home.

"Are you sure you don't want to come with me to my parents' place?"

Sasha placed her hairbrush down on the dresser and looked at Nick. "No, I'd only be in the way."

The Valente men were getting together at Cesare's apartment now that Alex was back from London. And Isabel was having Sunday brunch with a friend, so it was no use going with Nick just to sit and listen to the men talk business.

"You wouldn't be in the way," he said, a touch of gruffness to his voice.

Tenderness filled her but she tried not to show it. She'd accepted what he'd said about Brenda and it was forgotten. Now she just wanted to get on with her life.

With Nick.

"No, I've got lots of things to do here."

He went to kiss her then stopped to hover just above her lips. "So you're okay about Brenda?"

"Yes, I am."

And she was.

He kissed her then, a long lingering kiss that was meant to reassure her.

And it did.

Until she answered the phone an hour later and a woman asked to speak to Nick.

"He's not here at the moment," Sasha said, her fingers tensing around the handset. "Do you want to leave a message?"

"Tell him it's Brenda." The woman's pause was definitely for effect. "I'm returning his call."

Sasha held on to her composure. "His call?"

"Nick called me a little while ago and said to call him back. I thought it was from this number. This is his parents' old number, right?"

Her words implied that she knew his parents' number very well.

Sasha drew herself up straighter. "Yes, this was Cesare and Isabel's house. It's mine and Nick's now. I'll pass on the message that you called."

Her hands were shaking as she hung up the phone and for a moment she felt a silly sense of triumph. Then it hit her.

Nick had called Brenda.

To meet with her?

Or to tell her to leave him alone?

All at once Sasha's doubts rose again like weeds

in a garden. She tried to mentally cut them off at the roots but they went too deep.

Was Nick lying?

She'd believed him about not being in love with Brenda, but was she being a fool to be so accepting? Had she *wanted* to believe him because of her love for him? Had it blinded her to his faults? Made her weak to his lies?

No, she didn't want to believe any of that, but the scenario was all too familiar. Memories of her parents' marriage were always at the back of her mind, her father always so glib at assuring her mother he was working when he was out with his latest girlfriend. Her mother always accepting his assurances. Sasha was certain her mother hadn't always believed him, but she'd forgiven him anyway.

Was this the same situation between her and Nick?

Was she like her mother?

And was Nick more like her father than she wanted to admit?

All at once she had the urge to go see her parents. Perhaps by merely being around them she'd find she was just being silly.

An hour later her mother's eyes lit up with surprise when she opened the door. "Darling, what are you doing here?" she said, giving her daughter a kiss. "And where's Nick?"

"He had to go see Cesare about work," Sasha said, stepping inside.

"Men! Your father's not here either. He went into the office to fix something or other. On a Sunday, too!"

Sasha turned to hide her face so that her mother couldn't read the suspicion in her eyes. Was that just an excuse? Was her father out with his latest mistress?

"Anyway," Sally said. "It's just us girls today. We can catch up over coffee."

"That would be nice, Mum," Sasha said, regretting having come now. Instead of doubting her suspicions about Nick, this visit was only reinforcing that she could never be like her mother and so accepting of her husband's lies.

And if she couldn't trust Nick, then how could she stay married to him?

They chatted over coffee on the patio until Sasha's cell phone rang. It was one of the contractors handling the renovations. "Let me just get a pen and paper," she said, looking around for her handbag, remembering she'd left it on the kitchen table.

Sally waved her toward the study.

Sasha nodded and entered by the French doors, hurrying over to her father's desk. By the time she ended the call, she had the feeling this particular contractor was going to be more trouble than he was worth.

She sighed as she turned to leave and knocked

into the bookcase, causing a large vase to fall on the carpet and break.

"Oh no," she muttered, crouching down to pick up the pieces. She hoped it wasn't irreplaceable.

Suddenly she realized there was some rolled up paper in the vase that had now spilled out. She picked it up. Her father wouldn't be pleased to have his things all over the place, though why he would tuck them in a vase like this—

A shiver of apprehension slid down her spine as the paper unraveled and the name "Valente" caught her eye. She didn't mean to pry but the words "correct figures" had been written in pencil at the top of the paper.

Then she noticed another sheet of paper underneath it, looking like a duplicate of the top sheet except that the numbers were different.

She blinked, then reread them. Was she seeing what she thought she was seeing?

She swallowed hard. Oh God. It hadn't been enough for her father that she had married Nick. Porter had falsified the numbers to win the contract by undercutting the other tenders by one hundred thousand dollars. No wonder these papers were hidden away.

God, did Nick know? Was that why they'd delayed signing the contract a few weeks ago? She shook her head. No, if Nick knew he'd have done something about it.

Definitely.

"What are you doing with those?" her mother suddenly said in an accusing tone.

Sasha's head shot up, trepidation filling her. "You know, don't you?"

Sally rushed toward her and snatched the papers to her breast. "Know what?"

"That Dad falsified the numbers to win that latest contract."

"Don't be silly."

"Mum, I saw the paperwork. It's there in black and white."

Her mother flushed, then paled. "Darling, you can't say anything. Promise me you won't."

Sasha gasped. "I can't make a promise like that. What Dad did isn't only morally wrong, it's illegal."

Sally's face screwed up. "Yes, and he could go to jail. Oh dear God."

"Maybe he should have thought of that."

She grabbed Sasha's arm in desperation. "Darling, you can't do this to your father. He can't go to jail." She began to sob. "Besides, the deal's already—" another sob "—signed and delivered and—" sniff "—no one's ever going to know. Not unless you tell them."

"I can't *not* say anything, Mum."

"He's your father."

"Yes, and I'm married to a Valente."

"The Valentes have plenty of money. They won't miss this."

Sasha couldn't believe she was hearing this. "Mum, I can't—"

"Darling, look, don't do anything yet. Think about it all first. I'm sure you'll see that remaining quiet is the best thing."

"Mum—"

"Promise me, darling," her mother said, her voice getting shrill. "At least promise me you won't do anything just yet. Give me a chance to speak to him. I'll get him to pay back the money somehow."

Sasha was torn and confused and she just wanted to be alone for a while to think things through. "I don't know."

"Getting the contract freed up other monies and your father has the money to pay the Valentes back now. He'll have to find a way to do that without raising suspicion, but I promise he'll rectify the situation."

Could she believe that?

Did she even have a choice?

She sighed. "Okay, I won't do anything yet."

Her mother hugged her. "Thank you, darling, thank you. We'll sort things out, you'll see."

Sasha made a hasty exit after that. It was hard to believe her father had done such a thing.

It was even harder to believe her mother was sticking up for him.

Nine

"Something wrong?" Nick asked, watching as Sasha jumped slightly, her green eyes looking nervous all of a sudden.

"Wrong? Why do you say that?"

He'd been watching her over the top of his newspaper. "You were quiet during dinner and didn't eat much, and now you've been staring at the television like it has you under its spell."

A hint of pink stained her cheeks. "I find this show fascinating."

He looked at the television screen and saw they had gone to a commercial. "You were watching the news, Sasha, and I wouldn't exactly call the news fascinating. Interesting, but not fascinating."

"That's your opinion."

"Let's not quibble about words. Something's the matter." He hesitated to bring this up but "If it's about the party and Brenda—"

"It isn't," she dismissed without hesitation. "And I'm not giving that a second thought, okay?"

"Okay."

There was something definitely bothering her. She was too pale and not herself.

"I guess it's the renovations," she suddenly said. "There was a lot of work to be done in the initial stages."

Why did he have the feeling she was just saying that to stop him prying further?

"Is it too much for you?"

She looked horrified. "No! That wasn't what I meant. I love it. I really do. But with coming back from England, then the wedding, then working on the redesigning, I suppose I'm just a little tired tonight."

It made sense yet….

The news returned and she pasted on a smile that surpassed the false one on the newsreader's face. "The news is back on."

"Then don't let me stop you from being *fascinated,*" he drawled.

Her smile couldn't hide her wariness as she

returned to look at the screen. He still wasn't convinced there wasn't something troubling her.

He was even more convinced ten minutes later when he heard the telephone ringing out in the hallway and Sasha didn't move. She didn't even appear to hear it. Normally she would get up to answer it straightaway.

He was just about to do it himself when he heard Iris pick up the phone. Then the housekeeper popped her head around the door. "There's a telephone call for Mrs. Valente. It's her mother."

Apprehension crossed Sasha's face, then vanished. "Iris, please tell my mother I'll call her back later."

"Yes, Mrs. Valente."

Nick scowled as the other woman left. "You don't want to speak to your mother?"

She darted a look at him, then away. "I only saw her today. It can wait." She turned back to the television but there was a flush to her cheeks that gave her away.

Something was definitely wrong.

And it had something to do with Sally Blake.

Half an hour later he walked into the kitchen and found Sasha talking on the telephone.

"I said I wouldn't say anything," she was whispering, "and I won't. But—" Suddenly she saw him standing in the doorway and went pale. "Mum, er… I've got to go. Nick's just walked in." She hung up.

Nick leaned against the doorjamb and crossed his

arms. Her words had been a warning to her mother, not a comment.

"Is the hot chocolate almost ready?" he asked, reminding her why she'd come here in the first place.

"Wh-what? Oh yes. I was just about to make it." She hurried over to the refrigerator and took out the milk.

"Your mother has a problem?"

She darted him a look. "You heard?" Without waiting for an answer she turned and took some mugs out of the cupboard. "It's um…women's problems," she said, not looking at him now. "Nothing you want to know about."

So, she was using that age-old excuse, was she? How could he refute it?

"Nick, why don't you go back in the living room. I'll bring in the drinks shortly."

He nodded, then turned and let her be, but if she thought she'd convinced him that nothing was wrong then she was in for a shock. He fully intended to keep an eye on things. Sally Blake had a secret and Sasha knew what it was. And that was fine as long as it didn't impact Sasha too much.

But by her reactions, it did.

Sasha had a restless night until Nick growled and pulled her into his arms, where she promptly fell asleep.

But her thoughts returned as soon as she opened her eyes the next morning. Dear Lord, how could her father cheat Cesare that way? Not to mention the whole Valente family? How could he cheat his *own* family like that? It put her in a terrible position.

"How about meeting me for lunch today?" Nick suddenly said, doing up his tie. "You're coming into the city anyway to talk to your suppliers."

His words brought her back to the moment and Sasha rolled on her side and watched Nick finish dressing for work. He was so handsome. So virile. She loved him so much.

And she might have to give him up.

Oh God, this might be her last chance to spend time with her husband. Her world would fall apart soon enough.

She leaned up on one elbow. "I'd love to have lunch with you, Nick."

He looked pleased. "Good. Leo will come back and pick you up in a couple of hours. He can drive you around while you do your business."

"I can drive my own car."

"Leo's not doing anything until he takes me home again. You may as well make use of him."

Her lips curved upward. "Make use of his services? Yes, I think I can do that."

"Hussy," he murmured, kissing her before he left.

She lay there in bed, just letting her love for Nick

be a part of her. *He* was a part of her, and she would never doubt that again.

She had her mother to thank for realizing that. Going to her parents' place yesterday had shown her Nick was *not* like her father.

Nor was her parents' marriage the same as her own marriage. At first she'd been scared and had projected her fears onto Nick. Nick Valente would not do what her father had done. Nick was good and honest. He'd been open and aboveboard about everything. And despite Brenda's phone call, Sasha was convinced the other woman had just been trying to make trouble. If Nick had called Brenda then it had been for an honest reason. She'd bet her life on it now. Nick was to be trusted.

Her father was not.

She kept those good thoughts of Nick close to her heart for the rest of the morning. Hopefully having only good thoughts would keep the bad thoughts at bay.

"You seem to be enjoying the view," he said over lunch at the harborside restaurant.

Sasha turned to look at him with a smile. "Their menu boasts they have the most glorious view in the world. I was merely checking it out."

"And?"

She surveyed the Harbour Bridge and Opera House through the large glass windows. "I'd say their claim is well-supported."

He smiled, then, "So, what's on the agenda for the rest of the day?"

"I've got a couple more places to visit before I finish up."

He took a sip of wine. "By the way, how's your mother today?"

She dropped her gaze to her plate so he wouldn't see the panic in her eyes. She was sure he hadn't believed her last night about her mother's medical problems. If the positions had been reversed she wouldn't have believed him.

Taking a breath, she looked up. "I only spoke to her last night, so I don't think anything's changed since then."

His eyes had a speculative look. "Aren't you concerned for her health?"

"Of course, but it's nothing urgent. My mother will be fine." Time to change the subject. "By the way, you didn't tell me about the U.K. launch. Did it go well?" She'd been understandably preoccupied last night and had forgotten to ask him about it.

His gaze held hers for a second too long, as if he was considering why she had changed the subject. "It went very well by all accounts. We're launching it on the Continent next."

She was grateful he didn't mention Claudine and any upcoming launch in France.

"It's a gorgeous perfume, Nick."

"I notice you wear it a lot."

"It's my favorite."

"It's every woman's favorite."

She smiled at the usual show of Valente arrogance, and all at once he smiled back with the full power of a Valente smile. The breath hitched in her throat.

The waiter returned to refill their glasses, allowing her to mentally break free of Nick.

When they were alone again Nick said, "How would you like to go on a harbor cruise on Wednesday? We have some prospective customers visiting from the States and I need to take them out to lunch and show them the sights. They're only here for a couple of days."

For a second, sharp anxiety twisted inside her. Would her father have paid back the money by then? Or would she have to gather her strength for Friday's deadline? How *did* a person knowingly send their father to jail?

"The women aren't anything like Claudine," Nick reassured her, thankfully reading her hesitation wrong.

"It sounds like fun."

They ate in silence for a while, until Sasha's cell phone rang. She left it in her handbag, ignoring it and wishing she'd thought to put it on silent.

"Aren't you going to answer it?"

"No."

"It could be important."

Nothing was as important as lunching with Nick. Every second with him counted.

She gave an unconcerned shrug. "It's only about the renovations. I'll get to it later."

Her phone stopped ringing.

"Would you like dessert, madam?" the waiter asked, suddenly appearing at her side.

"Um…" Her cell started to ring again. She opened her handbag and went to turn it off, but not before she caught the number displayed. It was her mother.

"No, just coffee," she said, trying to appear unconcerned as she switched the phone off.

Nick asked for coffee, too, then glanced to Sasha, "Was it a contractor?"

Flustered, she said the first thing that came to mind. "What? Oh, no, it was just my mother. I'll call her back later."

Nick's eyes were full of questions. "I'd have thought you'd want to talk to her."

Oh hell. Was she giving too much away?

"It's not exactly a subject to be discussed over lunch," she pointed out.

Nick grimaced. "True."

Just then Nick's cell phone began to ring.

He glanced at it. "I don't know that number."

"Let me see." Her heart sank. "It's my mother."

He frowned. "Then it must be important if she's calling me," he said, handing it straight to her.

There was nothing for it except to answer the phone, but Sasha got a shock as she listened to her mother's tearful voice. Oh God, she shouldn't have ignored her previous calls.

"My father's had a heart attack," she whispered to Nick in an aside, then spoke to her mother again. "I'll be there as soon as I can, Mum." She finished the call.

"*We'll* be there soon," Nick said, gesturing to the waiter, and a few minutes later hurried her out to the waiting car. "What's his condition?"

"I don't know."

Could *she* have been the cause of this? Her mother would have had to tell him she knew. And having his daughter threaten him with exposure and probable jail would certainly cause him stress enough to have a heart attack.

Yet how could she *not* do something about what she knew, she wondered, feeling like she was shriveling up with stress herself as they headed to the hospital.

Nick squeezed her hand. "You know, my dad's heart attack looked bad at first but it ended up only being a mild one."

She'd forgotten about Cesare's heart attack. Suddenly she felt guilty. "Nick, you shouldn't have come with me. I appreciate it, but I don't want you to go through it all again with my father."

"Don't be silly, Sash," he said gruffly. "I'm your husband."

Warmth rose up inside her and she had to blink back tears. He'd called her "Sash"—the name he'd called her years ago. It was something she'd forgotten until this moment.

"He'll be fine." He pulled her close and she leaned into him, grateful for his presence, comforted by his arms around her, and the now familiar scent of him.

It was only as they were walking toward her mother in the waiting room that Sasha had a tense moment of apprehension. Would her mother inadvertently say something in front of Nick about how Porter had taken the news? Would she blame Sasha's ultimatum for all this? Nick would have to ask why.

"Mum?"

"Oh, Sasha," Sally cried and hugged her.

Sasha returned the hug, relief easing through her. It didn't look like her mother was about to barrage her with blame. "How is he?"

Sally moved back. "I don't know. They told me to wait here." She sniffed. "But it's been ages now and no one will tell me what's happening."

"I'll find out," Nick said ominously, spinning on his heels. "Stay here." He strode out the door toward the nurses' station.

Sasha led her mother back over to her seat. "Mum, what happened?"

Sally gave a shuddering sigh. "When your father got up this morning he said he had indigestion so he took some antacid and went off to work. The next thing I know…" her voice shook "…they called me to stay he'd been brought here in an ambulance."

"So you haven't seen him yet?"

"No."

"Mum, did you—"

Nick strode back through the sliding glass doors. "The doctor's coming out shortly to talk to us."

"Oh God," Sally said and started to sob.

They didn't have to wait long for the doctor, and Sasha put her arm around her mother's shoulders as he told them the news that it didn't look like it been a heart attack at all.

"We're running more tests, but it appears it wasn't."

"Thank God," Sally said.

"What could it have been, Doctor?" Sasha asked.

"I'm not sure. We'll be keeping him here overnight. He's in a private room and Mrs. Blake can stay with him, if you like?"

"Oh, yes," her mother said. "Can I see him, Doctor?"

"He's resting, but I don't see why not." He paused. "But only Mrs. Blake for now."

Sasha watched her mother and the doctor leave

the room. It was wonderful that her father was going to be okay, but he still had to face tomorrow.

And so did she.

"Nick, why don't you go back to work? I'll stay here with Mum until we know more."

His jaw set stubbornly. "No. You need me. I'll stay."

"Seriously, I'll be okay. Besides, it'll probably be hours." She leaned forward and kissed his cheek. "Thank you, but it's no use just sitting around here doing nothing. I'm fine."

His gaze rested on her. "If you're sure?"

"Yes. Now go." It would give her the chance to talk to her mother in private. Sasha couldn't imagine she *wouldn't* have told her husband about yesterday, but she needed to know for sure.

Hours later her father had been given a cautious all clear and Sasha was allowed in to see him, but in the end she didn't get to ask her mother anything. Sally wouldn't leave her husband's side.

And as Sasha looked at her father sleeping peacefully on the bed, she wished so much that it could have been different. If only her father was a different man…a different person.

If only he was a better husband and father.

If only she could love him more.

Sasha finally arrived home around nine and found Nick asleep on the sofa in front of the television.

She'd expected to be home much sooner, so that when he'd phoned her she had even insisted he go straight home and not come to the hospital.

Now, standing in the doorway her heart softened as she looked at Nick. He was such a part of her. He'd always been a part of her. It would be like losing a limb to do without him.

For a moment her vision blurred. She blinked back the tears and turned away to hurry to the kitchen. She wasn't hungry but Iris had put a portion of lasagna in the oven for her, so she'd have to make the effort to eat it.

But first she showered and changed into her silk nightgown and robe, then put the lasagna on a tray and took it into the living room.

Hungrier now than she'd realized, she turned the television down low while she ate her food and watched Nick sleep. She thought the smell of the food might wake him, but it didn't, and she was sipping at her decaffeinated coffee and deciding to cover him with a blanket when his eyelids lifted.

For a moment he looked disorientated. Then he sat up and ran his fingers through his hair. "Damn, I fell asleep, didn't I?"

She gave an understanding smile. "You were tired."

"What time is it?"

"Almost ten."

His eyes grew alert. "You must be exhausted yourself."

"I'm better now that I'm home." And she was.

He scrutinized her more. "How's Porter?"

"They'll keep an eye on him overnight, but they're confident it wasn't a heart attack."

His face relaxed. "See, I told you there was nothing to worry about."

"I know."

All at once his gaze noted her night attire, and the air stilled. His eyes burned into her, making her heart skip a beat. She waited for him to get to his feet and pull her into his arms.

Only, he seemed to withdraw. "I think I'll use a spare room tonight. You need your sleep."

Disappointment filled her. "I won't be able to sleep without you," she said, putting herself on the line…putting her heart on the line and hoping he didn't notice.

The light of passion flared in his eyes again but was banked as he stood up and held out his hand. "Fine. We *sleep,* and that's all."

Her heart expanded at his thoughtfulness. He wanted her yet was prepared to put her needs first. Or what he *thought* she needed.

Happy to just be able to share his bed, she put her hand in his and together they went up the stairs. He made no attempt to make love to her, but he held her in his arms until she fell asleep. And she found that was just as welcome as making love.

She was home.

And she was where she wanted to be.

Ten

Cesare phoned the next morning to see how Porter was doing and Nick put the phone on loudspeaker so both he and Sasha could talk while they were getting dressed.

"Dad, it wasn't a heart attack." Nick went on to explain.

"Grazie a Dio!" Cesare said with relief.

"We've just called the hospital and he's already been released," Nick continued. "Sally will look after him. I'm sure she'll make him take things easy."

"Yes, she's a good woman." Cesare paused. "Sasha, your father's a good man. He gives so much of himself to everyone. It would be a great loss if anything had happened to him. He's the consummate businessman."

Sasha wanted to choke. If only Cesare knew....

"Thank you, Cesare," she managed. "That's kind of you to say."

Cesare ended the call after that and Nick kissed her good-bye, but as he drew back he hesitated. "Are you sure you don't want me to get out of the harbor cruise tomorrow? Alex or Matt can step in."

Tomorrow was Wednesday.

Only two more days until Friday.

The thought of having to force her father's hand pressed down on her. She felt sick at heart over him cheating the Valentes out of money.

She schooled her features. "No. I'll be fine."

Nick held her gaze a moment more. "Okay. See you tonight."

"Yes," she said, putting on a brave face.

As soon as he left, she finished dressing. She would go see her parents. Now that she knew her father hadn't had a heart attack, he had to rectify the situation soon. She couldn't go on like this.

No one answered the front door when she rang the bell, despite her father's favorite music coming from inside the house. Then she realized it was coming from the back patio, so she went around the side and opened the gate.

To her shock, she found her father sitting on the lounger in the back garden, smoking a cigar and drinking whiskey. He looked like a man who was celebrating life.

Or something else?

Suddenly it hit her.

"Oh my God," she accused, seeing him jump with fright as she strode toward him. "You didn't have a suspected heart attack at all. You made it up."

The blood siphoned from his face, then he turned red. "Don't be stupid, child. Of course I didn't make it up."

"I don't believe you."

He stabbed out his cigar. "You think I'd put myself through all those medical procedures, not to mention worrying you and your mother, for the fun of it?"

"Yes! You were desperate. And you didn't give a damn about me or Mum." Sasha swung around when she heard her mother come out on the patio behind her. "Mum, I can't believe you were a part of this."

Sally's eyes widened in alarm. "Wh-what?"

"Leave your mother out of this. She didn't know."

Sasha gasped. "So it's true."

"Know what?" Sally said, looking from one to the other.

"That Dad faked his heart attack so I wouldn't tell the Valentes about his falsifying records."

"No!"

"He thought I'd feel guilty enough to overlook the fact that it wasn't actually a heart attack. No doubt he planned on milking it for all it was worth."

"Porter?" Sally whispered.

"Sally, don't look at me like that. I was only thinking of you. What will happen to you if I go to jail?"

"How magnanimous of you, Dad," Sasha snapped.

"Mind your own business, Sasha," he growled.

She stared hard at him. "You don't regret what you did at all."

"Of course I do."

She knew he didn't. He only regretted getting caught.

"Dad, unless you tell me here and now that you're going to make things right and pay back the money, I'm going to tell Nick what you've done."

He turned white. "You don't mean that."

"I do."

"But I'm your father."

"Emotional blackmail doesn't work on me anymore." She pulled back her shoulders. "Now tell me that you'll make things right, or I go tell Nick right this minute what you've done."

He blanched. "Okay, okay. I'll pay it back, but it might take me a couple of days."

"You've got until Friday." She turned and walked away, her heart so heavy she was surprised she could walk at all. She'd never had much love or respect for her father but she had even less now.

Of course, she wasn't fool enough to trust him. And how the heck was she going to believe him on Friday anyway?

Yet there was a bigger picture here.

How was she going to look Nick in the eyes for the rest of her life and pretend this wasn't between them?

Sasha could feel Nick looking at her throughout dinner but she couldn't seem to lift her spirits. A black cloud hung over her head. It was only a matter of time before it all poured down on her.

After they'd eaten and moved into the living room, she still couldn't relax. She couldn't get interested in the unfolding legal drama on television. She had enough legal drama of her own right now.

And she was terrified her mother would call and put pressure on her to give her father more time, or to beg her to change her mind. She didn't want the stress of even talking to her mother right now and certainly not in front of Nick.

An idea occurred to her.

"I think I've got cabin fever, Nick. Let's go out for a drink somewhere."

He blinked in mild surprise and put aside some paperwork. "Will one of the local pubs do?"

"Yes, there's some lovely pubs around here. And

can we turn our cell phones off, please? Let's not have any interruptions."

He shot her an odd look. "If that's what you want."

Half an hour later they were sitting in the corner at a local pub, sipping their drinks. The hotel was on the heritage listing as were many buildings in the Hawkesbury district.

"Any special reason for the cabin fever?" he asked, leaning back in his chair, his eyes watchful.

It sounded a ridiculous thing for her to say now. They'd been out of the house a lot lately and cabin fever was the last thing she'd have.

She wrinkled her nose. "I guess it's more that we haven't had much time to ourselves."

He nodded. "And all that with your father didn't help either, does it?"

She gave a silent gasp. "Wh-what?"

"With Porter being in hospital."

"Oh." She swallowed. "Yes."

His look sharpened. "You've been tense all night. Are you sure you're telling me everything? He's not taken a turn for the worse, has he?"

"No, he's fine." Panic bounced inside her. She had to get thoughts of her father out of Nick's mind and onto something else. Otherwise she might give herself way. "Brenda called me, you know."

He straightened in his chair. "What? When?"

"Sunday morning after you went to your father's place. She said she was returning your call."

The look in his eyes turned hard and dangerous. He would be a formidable enemy. "She did, did she?"

"So you didn't call her?"

"No." His gaze focused back on her. "Did you think I had? Is that why you didn't tell me before now? You've been worrying yourself sick about it."

"No, that's not it at all. I figured you just wanted to tell her to stay away from you."

"I'd already told her. And she knows the score. She was just trying to cause trouble." He stared at her. "And succeeded."

"No, she didn't." Brenda had tried to make her doubt Nick, but in the end she hadn't succeeded.

Nick's eyes were razor-sharp. "You've been upset all evening. In fact, you haven't been yourself since Sunday at the party."

Somehow she held it together. Sunday was when she'd learned what her father had done.

"I told you it's because of everything else." She swallowed past her dry throat. "I believe you, Nick. I swear I believe you."

He studied her face, taking his time to measure her words. Finally a gentle look came into his eyes. "Thank you," he murmured.

Her heart tilted inside her chest.

In the end they stayed for over two hours, talking

about nothing much in particular and listening to a folk singer. Sasha could feel the tension easing out of her as the wine took hold.

"I think that did us both good," Nick said on the drive home.

She leaned her head back against the leather seat and smiled sideways at him. "We should do it more often."

He chuckled. "I believe you're slightly drunk, Mrs. Valente."

"Enough to take the edge off my pain," she said without thinking.

His scowl was instant. "You're in pain?"

She bit her lip and thanked heaven he had to concentrate on the road. "I had a headache before," she lied. "I thought it was going to turn into a migraine."

He darted a look at her. "Do you often get migraines?"

"No." But she had the feeling she may well start after all this.

Without warning, he gave a crooked grin. "Don't worry. I'll kiss you better if it returns."

"Then it'll be worth it."

"Don't say things like that when I'm driving," he pretended to growl.

She just smiled.

They arrived home and he parked the car in the sweeping driveway, but something happened inside her as she watched him come round to open the passenger door. A sense of impending doom centered in her chest. Suddenly she had the feeling this was all coming to an end.

"Come on, milady," he drawled, holding his hand out.

She vaguely heard him. This moment was far more important than joking or teasing or anything else in this world. God, she loved this man. How could she ever tell him the truth?

She stood up and cupped his face with her hands. "Make love to me, Nick. Make me forget all my headaches."

He looked down at her, his brows drawing together. "What's all this about?"

"Nick, don't talk. I need you tonight. Make me yours."

He opened his mouth to speak, then must have thought better of it. He released his breath and lowered his head.

After that it seemed like they kissed all the way to the bedroom. And in the bedroom…dear God, in the bedroom…their lovemaking took on a poignancy she was sure Nick felt, too. There was a deeper focus in his eyes as he looked at her. A longer than usual pause as he entered her.

And when he made her *his*—perhaps for the last time—her heart hurt.

Eleven

Sasha's pace quickened as she stepped from the elevator and walked toward Nick's office in the House of Valente building just before noon. Her sense of impending doom from last night had alleviated by the time she woke this morning, making her realize it had mostly been the wine.

But not all.

There was still a heavy feeling inside her that she'd been trying to push aside all morning, and it hadn't helped that the hours had dragged until it was time to come into the city for the harbor cruise. She'd needed to keep busy.

And she'd needed to see Nick again. Hopefully being with the man she loved would help push away those demons and doubts riding on her shoulder.

"He's in the conference room," Nick's personal assistant said. "I'll just let him know you're here." She went to press the intercom.

"That's okay, Joyce. I can wait in his office."

"No, he said to tell him when you arrived. It's only the family in there anyway."

Knowing he was waiting for her filled Sasha with pleasure, more so when Joyce said to go straight into the conference room.

"Thank you." Sasha's steps were lighter as she continued along to the end of the corridor. The view of the harbor through the panel of windows called out to her and she was really beginning to look forward to the cruise today. The harbor breeze could be just what she needed right now, especially if she was sharing it with Nick.

"Come in," Cesare called out in response to her knock.

Sasha opened the door with a smile. She had to admit she really liked being a part of the Valente family. Growing up, she'd often been a little wary of Cesare but he was a good man and so were the others.

"Well, well," the older man in question said as she came toward three of the Valente men sitting at the conference table. Nick was standing at the window looking out, his back to her. "You're just in time."

Sasha's steps faltered at his tone. "I…am?"

Why hadn't Nick turned to face her?

"In time for what, Cesare?"

"For me to have your father arrested for fraud."

Sasha's heart dropped to her toes.

"We've found out what he's been up to. Did you think we wouldn't?"

Sasha couldn't find her voice.

"I can't believe Porter thought he could get away with it," Cesare continued. "Does he think the Valentes are stupid? And you were in on it, too, weren't you, girl?"

She gasped at the accusation, aware of three sets of eyes upon her, but the eyes that mattered—Nick's eyes—were still turned away from her.

"And I, fool that I am, wanted Nick to marry you. I thought you were perfect for my son." He gave a harsh laugh. "No wonder Porter wanted you to marry Nick, and no wonder you agreed to the marriage. If it was all in the family he'd get that contract, no questions asked. Of course you had to say no first, didn't you? That way you could dangle yourself as bait in front of Nick and—"

"Enough!" Nick spun around, his face taut as he glared at his father. "You're accusing Sasha without any evidence. You don't know she was involved in any of this."

"Then ask her, *figlio mio*," Cesare said. "Ask her, and then we will know."

She watched Nick hesitate, and felt like she'd been slapped in the face.

He doubted her.

Then he straightened his shoulders and walked toward her. "Sasha," he said, his voice quiet but firm, his eyes with a hint of pleading in them. "Please tell me you didn't know about any of this."

A moment crept by. The others receded into the background. There was her and Nick.

Only her and Nick.

And soon....

She trembled. "I...I...can't."

He sucked in a sharp breath.

"Nick, I—"

His glare silenced her. "No excuses."

"But—"

"This was your sick way of getting revenge, wasn't it?" Disgust filled his eyes now. "Very clever, Sasha."

"Revenge? I don't know what you mean."

"Remember that kiss in the gazebo? Remember how you thought I'd rejected you? You wanted to pay me back for that, didn't you? You wanted your revenge."

"No!" she whispered, her voice threadbare.

"Yes."

At that moment, she knew it was over. He wasn't prepared to let her explain any of this. He wasn't even prepared to ask if there were extenuating circumstances, nor give her the benefit of the doubt.

And could she really blame him?

Giving a small cry, she spun away and ran from the room. It was over.

"I'm sorry, *figlio mio,*" Cesare said, coming up behind Nick and putting his hand on his shoulder.

"Not as sorry as I am, Dad." Nick's gut was one big knot of pain. He'd trusted Sasha. Trusted her like he'd trusted no other woman.

He should have known she'd let him down.

Cesare's mouth tightened. "*Santo cielo,* I'm going to see Porter myself!"

Alex jumped to his feet. "No, Dad. We can handle this."

Cesare clenched and unclenched his hands. "I want to see his face. He was my friend, and now he's a traitor."

"You're getting upset, and that's not good for you. Matt and I will go see Porter. Let Nick take you home."

"No," Nick growled. "I'm going to see Porter." He had more than a vested interest in all this.

Alex nodded. "Then Matt can take Dad home."

Cesare complained but he was shaken and obviously realized it was best he not be there to confront his now ex-friend. He left with Matt, and Nick and Alex took off for the Blakes' house.

Sally turned white when she opened the door to them. It was evident she knew why they were here.

Porter was eating dinner, and he went white, too, as Nick and Alex strode into the dining room.

Alex spoke first. "Porter, I've come to tell you that we're filing charges for fraud against you."

Sally gave a wailing cry behind them, but they ignored her.

The older man's face screwed up. "So Sasha told, did she? I should have known not to trust that daughter of mine. She finds out a couple of days ago and threatens to blow the whistle unless I—"

Nick stiffened. "*What* did you say?"

Porter made a harsh sound. "I said my daughter was going to blow the whistle on her old man. Can you believe it?"

Nick looked at Porter. "Yes, I can." Then he looked at Alex, who nodded in understanding.

"Take my car," his brother said, tossing the keys at him. "I've got a lot more to say to Mr. Blake."

Somehow Sasha managed to find some semblance of control by the time Leo dropped her off at home. She'd never been more grateful for the dark glass panel between them as she huddled in the corner of the back seat, unable to stop the tears from flowing.

Iris took one look at her face and was full of concern. "Mrs. Valente, is there something wrong?"

Sasha almost laughed out loud. Everything was wrong. And nothing could make it right.

Not ever.

"Are you ill? Would you like me to call a doctor?"

Sasha headed for the stairs. "I'd just like to be alone, Iris."

The housekeeper was clearly reluctant to accept that, but inclined her head. "If you wish, Mrs. Valente."

"I do."

Sasha made her way to the bedroom, sick with anguish. She threw some water on her face, hoping the coldness would take away her inner pain, but knowing it was a losing battle. She was burning up inside, her despair like a flame inside her, growing higher and more intense. An iceberg could not put it out.

She knew what she had to do. Nick would no longer want her in his house or in his life and she wouldn't wait around for him to kick her out. He would be glad to see her gone. No doubt he would even get someone else in to oversee the redecorating.

Her throat tightening, she began to throw some of her things in a suitcase. She would get the rest later.

Or better still, leave them for charity. She wouldn't want any reminders of her marriage.

Just then there was a tap at the door and she swallowed a moan. "Come in."

The housekeeper's eyes widened when she saw the suitcase on the bed. "Um…your mother's on the phone, Mrs. Valente."

Sasha's nerves tensed. "I don't want to talk to anyone right now, Iris."

"She says it's urgent."

Sasha winced, then realized it was best to take the call. She felt too raw to give her mother the support she needed right now, but once she pulled herself together, she'd manage it in the future.

Somehow.

She picked up the phone. "Mum, I—"

"Sasha, how could you! You said you would give your father until Friday and now you've gone and told the Valentes. You've betrayed your own family."

She then went into a tirade about Porter going to jail and that her daughter had sent him there, and at that moment Sasha finally understood something. No matter what her father did, her mother would always make excuses for him.

And her daughter would come a poor second.

Sasha quietly hung up. Her mother was welcome to do what she wanted with her life, but *she* wasn't about to help her do that any longer.

It was over.

Just like her marriage to Nick.

There was only one place where she'd found a measure of peace before. She would go back to London. There was nothing for her here.

Nick drove home as fast as he dared. Last night when Sasha had begged him to make love to her, she must have known something was about to happen. She should have told him the truth. She should have said something.

Anything.

Then he remembered how she'd tried to tell him the truth back in the conference room, only he hadn't wanted to listen. He'd accused her of revenge.

Dammit all to hell.

He took the stairs two at a time, not believing Iris's words that Sasha had packed her things and gone. Then he saw some of her clothes missing from the wardrobe and the dresser now empty of her possessions.

And he felt empty deep inside.

So empty he wasn't sure if he could live without her. *Not when she'd taken his heart with her.*

He sucked in a lungful of air. He hadn't seen it coming, but he loved her. It hit him fair and square between the eyes. He could not deny it.

And now he couldn't even tell her. He had no idea where she'd gone, except that he knew she wouldn't go home. After what he'd seen, her parents wouldn't want her.

Well, he *did*.

He strode to the telephone beside the bed and called Joyce. He'd turn this city over until he found the woman he loved.

Twelve

Sasha tightened the belt of her bathrobe, then began toweling her hair dry as she walked into the bedroom. She probably should order something to eat except that she didn't have an appetite. It was going to be a long time before—

"Sasha."

Her head shot up, her heart slamming against her ribs at the sight of her husband standing in her hotel room. "Nick!"

Their eyes locked, but she could tell nothing from his expression.

"Yes, Sasha. It's me."

Her mind tried to take it in. He was here. Oh God, Nick was really here. But how? Why? She dare not hope. No, not even the tiniest bit.

Placing the towel on the table, she pushed back her wet hair and faced him. "How did you find me?"

"You used your credit card to book the hotel, and then again for your flight to London tomorrow."

She hadn't thought he'd be looking so she hadn't given it a second thought. Then she realized why he'd come looking for her. The disappointment was immense.

She thrust back her shoulders. "Look, if you want more details about my father, you've had a wasted journey."

"I already know the details."

Her forehead creased. Was he playing some sort of game with her? "Then there's nothing to say."

"There's plenty to say." He paused and suddenly regret seemed to cut through him. "I'm sorry, Sasha."

"S-sorry?"

"For not trusting you."

She swallowed hard. "I don't understand."

"I shouldn't have been so quick to believe you'd have anything to do with what your father did."

She searched his eyes. "You believe me?"

"*Now* I do. But it wasn't until Porter inadvertently told us your involvement that I realized I'd misjudged you." He took in a lungful of air. "I'm sorry, Sasha. I'll say I'm sorry every day for the rest of our lives if that's what it takes."

Her heart began to wobble. "You want me to come back to you?"

His expression opened up fully for the first time ever. "How can I live in that great big house without the woman I love to share it with me?"

"Nick, are you—" She moistened her mouth. Dare she say the words? "Are you saying you *love* me?"

"Yes."

Her heart jumped with joy but still she held back. She was too scared to believe it. There had to be another reason.

"Is this your revenge, Nick? Are you going to get me to admit I love you and then walk away?"

There was a flash of pain in his eyes. "No. The only direction I'm walking in is *to* you." His steps did exactly that. And then he stood in front of her, his gaze achingly intense. "Do you love me, Sasha?"

She looked up at him and could fight it no longer. "Yes, Nick, I do. I've always loved you. I always will."

He pulled her close. "Oh God, I love you, Sash," he said thickly, his deep voice caressing her ears.

"Nick," she murmured, love swelling within her.

He drew her close and kissed her. She inhaled him in like he was the very air, his heartbeat merging with hers, his touch purring along her skin, his scent mingling with her own. She'd never felt more alive.

Or complete.

He moved back but held her within the circle of his arms. "Last night I knew there was something going on with you, but I didn't know what. And today, I didn't know if you could forgive me." His lips brushed hers. "I just have to say it again. I love you."

"I'll never get sick of hearing you say it," she whispered, the love in his eyes stealing her breath. "I love you so very much, Nick."

He hugged her tight for a short while, then eased back. "I had some bad moments on the way over here, let me tell you."

"Perhaps I gave in too easily then?" she teased.

His lips twitched. "If you hadn't, I'd be a nervous wreck by now."

"You a nervous wreck? Never!"

"You're right," he said, making her smile at his Valente arrogance. "I'd never be a wreck because I wouldn't have let you go in the first place."

"I can't fault that reasoning."

His hands tightened on her waist. "Speaking of giving, you give so much of yourself, trying to balance it all so that no one will get hurt. Your parents don't deserve you. *I* almost didn't."

"Nick, I should have told you as soon as I could,

but I was torn. How could I be responsible for sending my father to jail?"

"You weren't responsible for anything."

"I was responsible to you as your wife. I should have made him tell you in the first place."

His mouth tightened. "Your father is the one who should have been responsible."

She winced, then, "You know, I'm glad it's over now. It would have always been between us because *I* would have known."

"I can guarantee it won't be between us now."

Her heart rolled over as she looked up at him. "Oh, Nick."

"Call me darling."

"Darling," she murmured. Then she remembered something else. "What about your family?"

"They'll know the truth by now. They won't hold anything against you."

"But Cesare—"

"Loves you like a daughter. It's the reason he was so hurt. He will apologize and no more will be said about it."

His words gave her joy. "I love your family, Nick."

"As long as you love me more."

"Oh, yes! Far, far more."

He glanced at the bed. "Seeing that you've already paid for the room…"

She arched one of her eyebrows. "Are you suggesting I go to bed with you, Nick Valente?"

"Do you have a better suggestion, my darling?"

"Not a one."

With their hearts finally open to each other, he drew her down on the bed beside him and at that moment she finally acknowledged something to herself. Loving Nick was no longer the worst thing that could happen in her life.

Loving Nick was the *strongest* part of her life.

Epilogue

Nick watched his very beautiful wife come toward him in the church and his heart swelled with love. He'd ruined Sasha's dreams seven years ago, and then almost ruined them again more recently. This time he was going to make sure her dream came true.

A lump formed in his throat when he saw her blinking back tears during the service. He never knew life could bring such happiness as he'd had the last few weeks with Sasha.

"Darling, thank you," she murmured after they walked back down the aisle past the Valente family, who were their only guests. "The church is so beautiful."

He'd searched high and low to find the perfect church for her and finally found it up in the mountains. The historic church had stained glass windows that looked out over the valley to the ocean where the heart of Sydney could be seen many, many miles away.

Outside the church his family…no, make that *their* family…gathered round to congratulate them and have their picture taken for posterity.

"There's one more thing I want to do," he whispered in her ear.

"What's that?"

"I'll show you later, my love."

And he did.

That night the moonlight shone over the silhouette of a couple kissing in the gazebo. And this time when Nick left to go back to the house, he wasn't alone.

He had Sasha by his side.

As it always would be.

* * * * *

*Harlequin is 60 years old,
and Harlequin Blaze is celebrating!
After all, a lot can happen in 60 years,
or 60 minutes...or 60 seconds!*

*Find out what's going down in
Blaze's heart-stopping new mini-series,*
FROM 0 TO 60!
*Getting from "Hello" to "How was it?"
can happen fast....*

Here's a sneak peek of the first book,
A LONG, HARD RIDE
*by Alison Kent
Available March 2009.*

"Is that for me?" Trey asked.

Cardin Worth cocked her head to the side and considered how much better the day already seemed. "Good morning to you, too."

When she didn't hold out the second cup of coffee for him to take, he came closer. She sipped from her heavy white mug, hiding her grin and her giddy rush of nerves behind it.

But when he stopped in front of her, she made the mistake of lowering her gaze from his face to the exposed strip of his chest. It was either give him his cup of coffee or bury her nose against him and breathe in. She remembered so clearly how he smelled. How he tasted.

She gave him his coffee.

After taking a quick gulp, he smiled and said, "Good morning, Cardin. I hope the floor wasn't too hard for you."

The hardness of the floor hadn't been the problem. She shook her head. "Are you kidding? I slept like a baby, swaddled in my sleeping bag."

"In my sleeping bag, you mean."

If he wanted to get technical, yeah. "Thanks for the loaner. It made sleeping on the floor almost bearable." As had the warmth of his spooned body, she thought, then quickly changed the subject. "I saw you have a loaf of bread and some eggs. Would you like me to cook breakfast?"

He lowered his coffee mug slowly, his gaze as warm as the sun on her shoulders, as the ceramic heating her hands. "I didn't bring you out here to wait on me."

"You didn't bring me out here at all. I volunteered to come."

"To help me get ready for the race. Not to serve me."

"It's just breakfast, Trey. And coffee." Even if last night it had been more. Even if the way he was looking at her made her want to climb back into that sleeping bag. "I work much better when my stomach's not growling. I thought it might be the same for you."

"It is, but I'll cook. You made the coffee."

"That's because I can't work at all without caffeine."

"If I'd known that, I would've put on a pot as soon I got up."

"What time *did* you get up?" Judging by the sun's position, she swore it couldn't be any later than seven now. And, yeah, they'd agreed to start working at six.

"Maybe four?" he guessed, giving her a lazy smile.

"But it was almost two…" She let the sentence dangle, finishing the thought privately. She was quite sure he knew exactly what time they'd finally fallen asleep after he'd made love to her.

The question facing her now was where did this relationship—if you could even call it *that*—go from here?

* * * * *

Cardin and Trey are about to find out
that great sex is only the beginning….
Don't miss the fireworks!
Get ready for

A LONG, HARD RIDE
by Alison Kent
Available March 2009,
wherever Blaze books are sold.

CELEBRATE
60 YEARS
OF PURE READING PLEASURE
WITH HARLEQUIN®!

**We'll be spotlighting a different series
every month throughout 2009
to celebrate our 60th anniversary.**

Look for Harlequin® Blaze™ in March!

0-60

*After all, a lot can happen in 60 years,
or 60 minutes...or 60 seconds!*

Find out what's going down in Blaze's
heart-stopping new miniseries *0-60!*
Getting from "Hello" to "How was it?"
can happen fast....

Look for the brand-new 0-60 miniseries in March 2009!

REQUEST YOUR FREE BOOKS!

2 FREE NOVELS PLUS 2 FREE GIFTS!

 **Silhouette® Desire®**

Passionate, Powerful, Provocative!

COMING NEXT MONTH
Available March 10, 2009

#1927 THE MORETTI HEIR—Katherine Garbera
Man of the Month
The one woman who can break his family's curse proposes a contract: she'll have his baby, but love must *not* be part of the bargain.

#1928 TALL, DARK...WESTMORELAND!—
Brenda Jackson
The Westmorelands
Surprised when he discovers his secret lover's true identity, this Westmoreland will stop at nothing to get her back into his bed!

#1929 TRANSFORMED INTO THE FRENCHMAN'S
MISTRESS—Barbara Dunlop
The Hudsons of Beverly Hills
She needs a favor, and he's determined to use that to his advantage. He'll give her what she wants *if* she agrees to his request and stays under his roof.

#1930 SECRET BABY, PUBLIC AFFAIR—Yvonne Lindsay
Rogue Diamonds
Their affair was front-page news, yet her pregnancy was still top secret. When he's called home to Tuscany and demands she join him, will passion turn to love?

#1931 IN THE ARGENTINE'S BED—Jennifer Lewis
The Hardcastle Progeny
He'll give her his DNA in exchange for a night in his bed. But even the simplest plans can lead to the biggest surprises....

#1932 FRIDAY NIGHT MISTRESS—Jan Colley
Publicly they were fierce enemies, yet in private, their steamy affair was all that he craved. Could their relationship evolve into something beyond their Friday night trysts?

SDCNMBPA0209